Last Stop Hotel

Michael David

Grosvenor House
Publishing Limited

All rights reserved
Copyright © Michael David, 2025

The right of Michael David to be identified as the author of this
work has been asserted in accordance with Section 78
of the Copyright, Designs and Patents Act 1988

The book cover is copyright to Michael David

This book is published by
Grosvenor House Publishing Ltd
Link House
140 The Broadway, Tolworth, Surrey, KT6 7HT.
www.grosvenorhousepublishing.co.uk

This book is sold subject to the conditions that it shall not, by way of
trade or otherwise, be lent, resold, hired out or otherwise circulated
without the author's or publisher's prior consent in any form of
binding or cover other than that in which it is published and
without a similar condition including this condition being
imposed on the subsequent purchaser.

This book is a work of fiction. Any resemblance to
people or events, past or present, is purely coincidental.

A CIP record for this book
is available from the British Library

Paperback ISBN 978-1-83615-190-6
Hardback ISBN 978-1-83615-191-3
eBook ISBN 978-1-83615-192-0

I would like to thank everyone at Grosvenor House Publishing for making my book possible. And I would like to dedicate this book to my agent, Melanie Bartle at GHP, who helped and supported me along the way. Your advice was much appreciated, thank you.

And who else? Oh, yes, and to my readers. Thank you, enjoy, and have a very pleasant life. What was that? I was laying it on too thick? Give me a break. I was trying to be nice…

A Crazy Life

I remember being a kid growing up in south-east London. I'd sneak into pubs with my friends, and they'd turn a blind eye. In the '70s, not even the cops were interested as long as we kept quiet and behaved ourselves, but back then nothing was predictable. In 1973, when I was 11, my family moved to a council estate in Lee Green. The local pub was a place called the Northbrook. When I was a youngster, I'd go in there, have a drink and watch the entertainment. I was shy and had problems socializing, but after a few, I was everyone's friend. I remember sitting at a table with the comedian Max Wall. He'd have a few and do his funny walk. Had us all in fits. And having a drink with Patrick Murray who played Mickey Pearce, the cockney conman in *Only Fools and Horses*. He had problems later with cancer. Rest in peace. He'd wander in occasionally and tell us funny stories. The punters loved him. There were plenty of jokers in the Northbrook and you were guaranteed a laugh. You've probably heard the saying fact is stranger than fiction. Well, I remember one time when they had trouble finding a landlord.

The Northbrook was owned by the brewery. Every few months they'd send a new landlord because the last one had to leave in a hurry. One landlord was only there a couple of hours. Someone knocked him out with a punch, and while he was sleeping on the floor everyone was serving themselves. "And don't forget the till and the smokes." So, the brewery sent another landlord. And people used to roll joints on the bar and get Rizlas behind the counter. You'd see the bar staff walking around stoned. I don't know how they did their job. If you were an idiot, you were in good company. I went there for the free booze and a bit of work and kept out of trouble. A couple of years later, there were bouncers on the door.

I know what you're thinking: *people can't be that stupid*. I knew a dealer that used to drive around stoned. When the cops pulled him over for dangerous driving they found two kilos in his car. It's a good job he wasn't working for the Columbians. He'd be lying in some wall. And there's a saying in London: where there's mugs, there's villains. Some of the pubs in London serve stolen goods behind the bar, or they know a man you can go to.

You just whisper in the bar guy's ear, "I'll have a pint, and I'm looking for a TV." And he'll tell you to come back later.

And if you want drugs, he'll point to a dealer. "See that fella over there." And he'd get a commission from the dealer.

I don't know what the pubs are like in your area, but in those days, London pubs were run by villains and somebody else's name was on the door. The cops knew what was going on, but long as they got paid, who's judging who. And they'd get a free drink from the tap. "Hey, snap my picture with Ronnie Biggs here." I know, you can't make up this bullshit. I look at the trouble in some of these areas with drugs and booze and I'm not surprised.

You've probably heard the story. Two strangers sitting in a bar. One turns to the other and tries to impress him about how important he is. He's done this and that and knows a lot of people. So, the other guy gives him a funny look. "So, what's it to me?"

"Just wanted you to know I can get any drugs you want."

So, the other guy brought out a badge and told him, "That's good to know."

I know, every pub has one. Don't get me started. Before we had social media, we had word of mouth. In London, people were known by reputation. The Criminal Wall of Fame. If you didn't hear about a face, they weren't worth knowing. I remember sitting in a pub watching the villains come through the door with their birds. They thought they were movie stars. They were admired and respected. Everybody wanted to be one.

"Is that who I think it is?"

"Yeah, a legend in his own mind."

But if you smiled and played along, they were good for a few drinks. Like the saying goes, 'a fool and their money'. And the people they were trying to impress were cretins just like them. Then they'd disappear for a while, and you'd hear they were in prison. Just another forgotten legend. The glamorous life of a crook.

You're probably thinking, *this guy's clued up. He should have been a criminal psychologist.* Joking! The crime rate would go up. I've been here a long time, but I'm still bumping into things.

Once I got a job as a security guard watching an old building at night. I was the only one there and thought the place was haunted. It gave me the creeps. First week on the job, my boss turned up on the site and saw me gone. He found me later in the pub. I was fired on the spot. And I got another job behind a bar. It was the landlord's night off. People came in, bought a drink – "And get one for yourself." The landlord came in later and found me unconscious on the floor. Money was gone and the place had been raided. I was sleeping, so it wasn't me. Lost that job too.

I remember going into the job centre before I signed on sick. I'd be half-cut with a bottle in my pocket. They can't bar you from drinking. They'd look at me and shake their heads like I was a lost cause. They were happy I was gone. I'm not proud of it, but I was a hopeless drunk.

Yeah, and there's more bullshit. I've met some characters in my life. Some of them I'm embarrassed to talk about. Alcohol is like a truth-teller. It lowers the inhibitions and brings out your true self. I've seen gentle people turn nasty under the influence. I knew this little old man who wouldn't hurt a fly. The sweetest guy you could meet, but after some Gold Label, he was Jekyll and Hyde. I was drinking with him and another guy. Just a regular Saturday night. After a few drinks he wanted to fight everyone. I thought it was funny, but the other guy knocked him out with a punch. It was like a Popeye movie. I couldn't believe it! I thought he was dead! I made my excuses and got out of there fast! I know, naughty, naughty. Should have stuck around to make sure he was alright, but I was drunk. Anyway, I saw him the next day and he was okay. Didn't even remember it. It was crazy. But for me alcohol had the opposite effect. It made me stupid and funny. Some like being around a crowd, but my biggest fear was shopping and crowded places, but once the alcohol hit me, I didn't have a care in the world. And I always had a bottle of Dutch courage in my bag. Like the American Express advert. Never leave home without it. I remember drinking some White Lightning cider. That stuff will turn you into a zombie. And it was cheap. Talk about rocket fuel. I'm lucky I still have a brain to think with.

Once I was living in Great Yarmouth, drinking with some bums. One of them had cirrhosis of the liver from years of booze. His stomach was so big. He looked like a beached whale. The doctor warned him to stop drinking, but he didn't care. He used to joke about dying. Then one day he got his wish. A group of us were drinking in his living room when he fell asleep and didn't wake up. The ghouls gave him a minute's silence and carried on drinking. Life goes on. It was like a Guy Ritchie movie. I don't know about you, but I get a little paranoid drinking with a dead body. I thought, *what am I doing here?* These idiots were brain dead. That could be me lying there, and the only thing we had in common was the booze. It was a wake-up call. Adios, amigo, time to jog on. So, I hopped on a train and went to Colchester. Stayed a few nights in a night shelter, and they moved me onto bedsits and flats. The last place was like living on Elm Street. And the neighbour thought he was Freddy. I couldn't sleep at night. Thought he was staring at me through the wall. I spent ten miserable years there, then got out before I ended up in a mental hospital. Gave the landlord one week's notice and went to Suffolk. That fucker was sad to see me go. Who was going to play with Damien? I now live in a nice place with friendly people. And I've been sober and drug clean for more than ten years.

Some people say ignorance is bliss, but that's bullshit. I left school at 15 with no qualifications. I was illiterate until middle age. Then it hit me how dumb I was. If you're an idiot, people treat you like an idiot. Lacking an education made it difficult to survive. So, I taught myself to read and write. I told myself if others could do it, so, could I. People like ex-slave Frederick Douglas in the 19th century who became a journalist, and a leader for human rights. He helped free slaves during the American Civil War. And Malcolm X who taught himself how to read and write in prison. He showed the world that a man can change despite everything going against him. But I was more of a Martin Luther King kind of guy. Peace, love, and integration. Some think you need a classroom for an education, but all throughout history there are many great people that have educated themselves and have proved that education isn't solely dependent on an institution. It's determination, self-motivation, and our thirst for knowledge that inspires us to learn. And given the right environment, we all have the capability to improve our minds. And now I can read and write fluently.

At a certain age, you start to realize that being dumb isn't an easy life. You make bad choices and get involved with the wrong crowd. But now my eyes are open. Many underestimate the value of a good education. They think its only purpose is to find work. But there's more to life. A good education teaches us about people and the world around us. And enables us to understand ourselves.

A lot has happened in my life, but I don't dwell on the bad stuff. I keep a positive mind and make light of a bad situation. People may knock me for having a sense of humour, but humour gets you through the day. And as they say, if you don't laugh, you'll cry.

I look around and see the kind of world we're living in. People have stopped caring. We've become insensitive and have forgotten what it's like to be human. People see autistic people as lacking in empathetic intelligence, but when it comes to people and emotions, they see things from a different perspective and have a clearer understanding. Back then, I didn't have the intelligence to make sense of who I was. My environment lacked the care and provisions for people with a disability like mine. So, I acquired my wisdom and understanding from my experiences and mistakes. And drinking was just a way to cope. I'm not proud of some of the things I've done, but that's the way it was. You can't change things so don't dwell on it. Learn from your mistakes and turn your life around.

If you don't drink, it may be difficult to understand why people feel the need to drink. Some do it to get wasted and forget, but I drank to help me with my autism. To help me cope. I'm not criticizing alcohol and saying it's good or bad. When you've had a hard day, you need something to unwind. But it's being responsible enough to control how you behave. And knowing when to stop. It was destroying my life, so I had to quit. When I first started drinking it gave me a nice buzz, and the confidence to face people, but it was only short-term. Then I became dependent on alcohol and needed it to survive. And then there was the misery of supporting the habit. Most of the time it was a desperate struggle.

I'd be wandering the street with the shakes fretting about the next drink. Trust me, you don't need it. It was suicidal. Some think being a drunk is a glamorous life. Well, we live and learn. Anyway, take care and have a good life.

I knew a guy who thought he was King Tut. Instead of getting on with folks and enjoying life, he had to prove he was better than them. People meant nothing to him. They were just a nuisance that got in his way. So, he made life difficult for himself and ended up a lonely and bitter person. They say too much ego can warp your mind. If you get like that, put a bullet in your head. Hey, I was only joking! Put down the gun!

Here's a story about two bank robbers, a haunted hotel, and a full moon. Has anyone got any popcorn? Enjoy…

Last Stop Hotel

Me and my baby had just robbed a bank and were on the run from the law. As she drove the getaway car, my baby was like a demon behind the wheel. I had to tell her to slow down. "Take it easy, baby, I think we've lost them."

"You think? Those cops are like cockroaches around every corner!"

"I'm sure. Now let's dump the wheels and get another and make like a couple of tourists."

"Anything else, my lord and master?"

"And cut the wisecracks."

My boss gave us directions to a hideout. A hotel that catered for wanted criminals, and we were told to bring plenty of dough. I looked at the loot on the back seat and smiled.

"Is it far?" asked my baby.

"Keep going. We'll be there soon."

"Are you driving?"

"Let me know when you're tired."

So, we hijacked another car and left the owner floating in the river. Thanks, buddy. Then took turns at the wheel and slept in the car. When we got near our destination, we dumped the wheels and went the rest of the way on foot. It was night as we crept through the forest. I looked at the map and pointed. "Couple of miles that way."

"Are you sure?"

"Trust me."

She gave me a funny look. "That's what I'm afraid of."

I pushed her forward. "Quit yapping and start walking."

"Well, if it doesn't pan out, it was nice knowing you."

My baby made me smile. "Always the optimist."

As we cleared a path through some trees, we saw an old mansion with lights in the windows, surrounded by a big garden.

My baby pointed. "Is that it?"

I looked at the map. "It appears so."

"Doesn't it seem a little remote?"

"That's the whole idea."

"Who owns it?"

"I never ask questions."

"Why not?"

"Wise guys get killed."

She gave me a worried look. "You know what they say about the dumb leading the blind. When I'm with you, I don't know which is which."

"Relax, baby, what's the worst that could happen?"

She brought out her gun. "Let's go and find out."

I told her to put it away. "They might get the wrong idea."

"One day, I'm going to regret trusting you," she told me, putting it away.

So, we went to the door like a couple of honeymooners and rang the bell. It played an eerie tune that put a tingle in my toes. My baby trembled by my side. The door opened and an old man in a black suit, who resembled Lurch, greeted us. Maybe he was dressed for Halloween.

"How may I help you?"

My baby went to walk away, but I pulled her back.

"Hi." I smiled. "I believe you're expecting us. My boss booked us a room."

He asked for our names. So, I gave him fake ones.

He looked around. "Are you alone?"

I raised the bag of loot. "Just us and a few friends."

He stepped aside to let us through and showed us into a large room and told us to wait. "I'll get the master."

When he was gone, my baby gave me a funny look. "Do they still say master?"

"He's a servant and servants have masters."

"Remind me again when we meet Count Dracula."

My baby was a racket. "Relax, baby, soon we'll be sailing in the Bahamas with new identities."

"Well, if I end up like him, I'll shoot myself."

I told her, "If you end up like him, I'll do it for you."

"I bet you would."

The ghoul came back with a middle-aged guy in a black suit who looked like somebody's dead uncle. What was with all the black suits around here? Were they in mourning?

He held out a hand. "I believe you're looking for a room?"

I shook it. "We got your invitation."

"Your friend is a valued client. How long would you like to stay?"

I told him a couple of weeks, maybe three.

"And you understand that we only take cash?"

I raised the bag of loot and told him, "Wouldn't have it any other way. Want me to settle now?"

"When you leave. Would you like something to eat?"

"I'm famished." I turned to my baby. "What about you?"

She told me she could eat a horse. So, he took us into a large dining room and sat us at a table. "Someone will come to serve you shortly."

As we waited, my baby told me, "Remember that house on haunted hill? It has nothing on this place."

"Would you like to take your chances out there?"

"Maybe we'd have better odds. So, what's the plan?"

"I know a guy that can get us out of the country."

"Let me guess, you know a guy that knows a guy?"

A man appeared by our side like an apparition and almost made us jump.

"Where'd you come from?"

He ignored the question and gave us a menu. We ordered, then he went back to the kitchen.

He came back with our meals and place them on the table.

I asked, "Where is everyone? Are they playing hide and seek?"

"They've retired to their rooms, sir."

My baby looked at her watch and gave him a funny look. "This early? It's only 10:15."

He went away as silently as he arrived.

I told her, "Maybe they have an early start."

My baby shook her head. "Yeah, I wonder what time they rise up in Hell?"

After the meal, I complimented the chef. It put us in good spirit and made us forget all our troubles.

I tipped him a hundred. "Hey, when you're through here. Come work for me."

But he shook it away. "Your money's no good here."

"You do buy things?"

He just looked at us with vacant eyes, then walked away.

My baby played around with her food. "Did you check for poison?"

You've heard the saying 'be careful what you wish for'. My baby was wearing me down. "Are you ready for bed?"

As if on cue our host appeared.

"Man, with those Hush Puppies, you'd make a good cop."

"Can I show you to your room."

As we creaked along the passage, I asked, "Are these floorboards alive?"

I get how some people are unresponsive, but this guy was like the walking dead.

He opened the door. "Breakfast will be at eight in the dining room." And left us.

As we sat on the bed, I asked my baby, "So what do you think?"

"I'll let you know if we wake up in the morning."

"Yeah, you do that."

"Did you see the movie where a couple book into a haunted hotel?"

I told her it was a good film.

"It didn't end well."

I shook my head. My baby made me laugh. "Maybe you should swap trades. You'd make a good comedian."

"Let's sleep."

"Don't you want to make love?"

"It's been a long day and I'm tired."

I showed her a sad face. "And my baby needs her beauty sleep."

"Shut up and hit the sack."

"Yes, ma'am."

So, I switched off the light and got into bed.

I was woken by a tapping on the door. When I opened my eyes, my baby was wide awake beside me.

"Did you hear that?"

My mind was somewhere else. "Maybe someone got lost?"

"Yeah, looking for the toilet with an axe."

"You've got an overactive mind."

"Then go and see."

"You go."

"You go."

"No, you go."

"Let's both go together."

So, we got our guns and went to the door.

When I tried the door, it was jammed.

My baby looked like a punk on angel dust. "That's it, we're shooting our way out of here!"

I told her to relax. "Maybe it's stuck."

When I tried it again, it opened.

My baby had a crazy look in her eyes. "Someone's fucking with us!"

When I checked outside, the corridor was dark and empty.

"Who's there?" I called. No answer.

I turned to my baby and shrugged.

She gave me that look. "Did a ghost knock the door?"

"Maybe it was nothing."

"Well, let's walk around and make sure."

So, I told my baby to stay close and went out the door.

My baby tapped me on the back with her gun. "I'm right behind you."

I pushed it away. "And watch where you're pointing that thing."

As we went through the passage, a light from the full moon filtered through an un-curtained window.

My baby was shaking behind me. "If there's a monster, I'm shooting you first."

"Then you'll have no one to share the loot with."

"Don't tempt me."

As we carried on walking, I tried a few doors, but they were locked. And then we heard a howling noise like a wolf baying at the moon.

We froze.

My baby looked over my shoulder. "What was that?"

I shrugged. "Probably the wind."

She looked at me like I had rocks in my head. "Can the wind howl?"

My baby was giving me the heebie-jeebies. "Stay close, I got this."

"If we get out of this, I never want to see you again."

As we carried on walking, there were more howling. Then it stopped.

My baby gave me a funny look. "There's howling and everyone's still sleeping. Doesn't that seem a little strange?"

"Maybe they're deep sleepers?"

"Yeah, too deep."

I handed her the bag behind me. "Here, take this while I go and investigate."

When I was still holding the bag, I looked around. My baby was gone!

"Baby, where are you?" But I was greeted with silence.

"Stop messing around! Where are you?"

Only the haunting silence, then the howling started again.

"Who's there?" I cried, waving the gun around.

More howling and scratching like claws scraping the walls.

This shit was creeping me out! "Hey, stop fucking around! Who's there?"

More howling and scraping.

I wanted to start blasting, but didn't want to waste bullets. "Come out and show yourself!"

Scrape, scrape, scrape, and more howling.

"Come out, fucker, wherever you are!"

Scrape, scrape, scrape, scrape.

I had a mind to hot toe it out of there, but where to? So, I cried at my tormentor, "You can run, but you can't hide!"

A shadow passed in front of me. Then it was gone.

Yeah, who was I kidding? I was imagining all kinds of crazy shit! Warm liquid was coursing down my pants. So, I screamed, "Alright! Alright! You win! I give up!"

But the howling and scraping came closer.

That crazy fucker was taunting me! I couldn't take anymore! So, I threw the bag and screamed, "Take it! Take it! It's yours! And keep the girl! Just let me go!"

Then, out of nowhere, something big knocked me down, and sharp claws struck my back and made me yell like a motherfucker! Then the thing turned me over and sat on my chest. A large hairy beast with sharp teeth and monstrous eyes was staring down at me, dripping saliva onto my face. When I tried to raise the gun, the claw held down my arm, and it shook its head. Naughty, naughty.

I told the creature, "There's dough in the sack. It's yours if you let me go."

But it was bullshit and the creature knew it. It had me and the dough. What do they say, you can bullshit your friends, but you can't bullshit a monster. Well, it was a nice life.

"Mind if I have a smoke before I go?"

The werewolf smiled and snapped its fangs at my face like it was toying with its food. Then it spoke in a blood-curdling voice, "Welcome to the last stop hotel."

---- *END* ----

It's a horror comedy like the *Creepshow*. When I wrote it, I thought about the movie, *From Dusk till Dawn.*, about two fugitives running from the law and ending up in a vampire bar in Mexico. It gave me the heebie-jeebies. I get how crooks are desperate not to get caught, but you'd have to be crazy to get yourself in that situation.

We appreciate our freedom and see it as our right. Shouldn't others be allowed to live free? How would you feel if someone took away your freedom. You would call it an inhuman act of cruelty. Yet, people are hypocritical when it comes to dictators. So, I'd like to remind you: we shouldn't wish on others what we wouldn't wish on ourselves.

The Thin Blue Line

In Boston, a detective was investigating a gang of rogue cops that were executing crooks. He was flying solo on a mission from his captain. Then one day he went missing. The captain informed his family, and the family contacted the brother who was a detective sergeant in Brooklyn PD.

Brooklyn, New York, Detective Sergeant Jacob Brown of the Robbery Homicide Division knocked on the captain's door and was told to enter. The captain offered him a seat.

He remained standing and nodded. "Sir."

"We're all concerned about Luke," said the captain. "But there could be an innocent explanation for his disappearance."

"That's what I aim to find out, sir."

"You've got some vacation time. I hope you find him."

"And if I need more?"

"Give me a call."

"Thank you, sir. Will that be all?"

The captain dismissed him. "See you when you come back."

Brown nodded and left the office.

He stepped out the station, got into his car and went to his apartment, packed a bag, then drove 200 miles to his family home in Boston. His mother met him at the door and took him into the house. They walked into the sitting room and met his father standing by the fireplace. He held out a hand and greeted his son. They shook and sat down. Jacob sat opposite his father's chair on a couch.

"Are you hungry?" asked his mother.

Jacob shook his head. "I'm good for now."

"Can I get you a drink?"

He shook his head.

They hugged, and she sat next to him.

"Have they heard anything?" enquired his mother.

He told them he would know something later.

His mother asked if he was staying.

Jacob told them he had found a hotel.

"There's plenty of room here," said his father.

"It's paid for and I'm going to be busy."

"You, sure, son?" asked his father.

Jacob got up to leave. "I'll come by later."

They said goodbyes. Then Jacob left and drove to the hotel. Made some calls. Then drove to the precinct where he met Lieutenant Matt Jennings.

The lieutenant took him into his office and sat behind a desk. He offered Jacob a chair. "You're here about your brother?"

"Any news on Luke?"

"He hasn't reported back yet, but he's a good detective. I'm sure he'll turn up."

"Has he gone absent before?"

Jennings shook his head. "But there's a first time for everything. Don't worry. We're looking out for him."

"When was Luke last seen?"

"He's been gone a week, but it's early days. Go back to Brooklyn. We'll keep you informed."

"I've got a few weeks leave. I'm spending it with my family. Mind if I ask around?"

"As long as you're discreet and no gun and badge."

"I'm leaving them at home."

"And don't break any laws."

Jacob nodded.

"Where are you staying?"

Jacob gave him the name of the hotel.

"Mind if I speak with his partner?"

"I'll see what I can do."

They spoke for a while and shook hands. Then Jacob went to speak with his brother's partner, Detective Daniel Snow.

They sat at a table, opposite each other in a room.

"Mind if I smoke," said Snow, bringing out his cigarettes.

"Feel free."

He offered Jacob a smoke, but he declined.

"When did you last see Luke?"

"Last week, Tuesday."

"Were you working a case?"

"It's an ongoing investigation, but I'm sure it has nothing to do with his disappearance."

"How do you know?"

"I know. Let's leave it at that. He probably with some broad somewhere having the time of his life. Boy, now you're making me jealous."

"Has he got a girl?"

"What am I, his chaperone?"

"Just trying to get a feel on my brother."

"We haven't been partners long."

Jacob knew he wouldn't get anywhere. So, he held out a hand. "No hard feelings."

"None taken," said the detective, shaking his hand.

"Can I call on you again?"

The detective nodded. "I'll be around. And don't worry. When he shows up, you'll be the first to know."

They exchanged cards and Jacob left the room. He drove around to places his brother frequented and spoke with people he knew.

Two crooks, Saul and Josh, were drinking and negotiating a deal. Drugs for guns. Josh snorted a line of coke and offered the straw to Saul, but the gun runner declined.

"Give me the gossip."

"I hear someone's killing off the competition."

"More business for me."

"I hear they're coming after you."

Saul took a drink from his glass. "So, we hit them first."

"I've got no beef with them. They're after you."

"And anyone associated with us."

"Then we better cut ties."

Saul gave him a hard look. "Then you become the enemy."

"I thought we were friends?" said the dealer, looking wounded.

"Friends don't bail on each other."

Josh looked up from snorting a line. "But that wasn't the deal."

"Deals have a way of changing."

"You're fucking with me. What can I do?"

"Find out who these clowns are," said Saul. "Like your life depended on it."

Matt, Snow, Bruno, Harlan, and Nancy had suspended their operation until Jacob was gone. They were relaxing by a pool in the garden of a big house. The men were in shorts, and Nancy was in a bikini. They took their drinks into the house and sat around a table.

Harlan told the others, "The brother's giving me a headache."

"Want me to whack him?" said Bruno, smiling.

Everyone except Matt, laughed.

"Don't even joke about it," Matt told them.

"So, what do we do?"

"We take it easy for a while."

"He could hurt us," said Nancy. "Maybe we should arrange an accident?"

"We don't hit our own," Matt told them.

"What about Luke?"

"That was an accident."

"Let's get out while we can," said Harlan. "This could blow up in our face."

"Chill out, nigger," Bruno told him. "And let the grown-ups handle this."

"Who are you calling a nigger? I work for a living."

"Well, work on this," said Bruno, taking out his cock.

The others laughed.

"Fuck you!" said Harlan. "Fuck all of you!"

"Yes, please!" said Nancy, smiling.

More laughter.

Matt told them, "We ride it out. He'll be gone soon."

But Nancy wasn't happy. "I say we do him and be done with it."

Harlan looked nervous. "I didn't sign up for this."

Matt felt the tension and it was making him uneasy. "And bring heat on our head. Way to go, Nancy. We wait until he's gone. End of discussion."

The others agreed.

Jacob drove to his brother's previous partner's address and parked in front of a house. He rang the bell and a man in his 60s answered the door. Jacob introduced himself and enquired if he was Frank Olsen.

The man told him he had the wrong place.

"I'm here about my brother and I was told you were friends."

The man stepped aside and invited him into the house and showed him into a room.

"What's it about?"

"He's missing and I'm trying to find him."

"What do you mean, missing?"

"He's been gone a week, and no one knows where he is. You were close once. I thought you might know."

"We were partners for eight years. I've been retired for two. I'm out of that life."

"And you don't keep in touch?"

"We exchange Christmas cards, and I mind my own business."

"I thought maybe you might be concerned."

"Can I get you something to drink, Detective?"

Jacob asked for coffee just to be polite. "Milk, no sugar. Thanks."

He left the room and came back with two cups.

He gave Jacob a cup. "He was here about six weeks ago."

"Did he mention anything about what he was doing?"

"Just needed some advice."

"About what?"

"He wanted to know what I would do if there were crooked cops in the department. I told him to mind his own business."

"Did he mention names?"

"He seemed nervous. Wouldn't talk about it. I told him to leave it alone. It would hurt him and the department."

"What did he say?"

"He said he'd see me later and left."

"He left?"

"I let him go. Look, I'm just an old man. I can't afford to be making waves."

"I understand, but do you know where he went?"

"If I did, I'd tell you. Look, I'm just a tired old man looking to enjoy his pension."

"Sorry I've troubled you."

"Wish I could do more."

Jacob held out a hand. "You've been helpful. Thank you."

They shook.

"Hope you find him. Leave me your number. I'll call if I hear anything."

Jacob gave him a card.

Have a nice day," said Jacob, leaving the house.

He got in the car and drove to the precinct.

As he approached the building, Bruno was by the door, smoking a cigarette.

He blew smoke passed his face. "Find what you're looking for?"

"Sorry, who are you?"

"Just a cop."

"Well maybe I'll see you around."

"You're the kid's brother, right?"

"You mean Luke?"

"Call a spade a spade."

"Still searching for the body," Jacob told him.

"Presuming he's dead?"

"Or maybe he's walking around the desert with amnesia."

Bruno shook his head and looked at him like he was a wise guy. "Go back to Brooklyn. You're not wanted around here."

"You got a problem with my brother?"

"Have you got a problem with me?"

"You should be nice. We're Indians in the same boat."

"Well, little Indian, keep out of my fucking way!" said Bruno, walking back into the building.

Jacob followed him into the precinct and met Matt at reception.

Matt led him through the squad room into his office. "I see you've met the resident clown."

"Every city has one."

"So, how are you settling in?" asked Matt.

"Lepers have better company."

Matt laughed. "The guys are not used to having a bigshot around."

"Is that what they're calling me?"

"You have an impressive record. There's a bar down the road. I get off in ten minutes. Want to join me? I'll introduce you to some of the guys."

"You, buying?"

"The first one's on me."

Matt took Jacob to a cop's bar. As they got to the counter, Bruno was leaning on the bar.

He gave Jacob a mean look. "I thought I told you to keep out of my way."

"He's with me," Matt told him. "Can I get you a drink?"

"I drink better alone," said Bruno, moving along the bar.

"I bet he's a charm with the ladies," Jacob told Matt.

"Takes a little getting used to. Pay him no mind."

They talked about Luke, then Matt introduced him to some guys. And they moved around the bar, small-talking and shaking hands. Matt was a popular guy. Jacob stepped outside for some fresh air and met Bruno smoking by the door.

"You don't hear so well!" Bruno growled at him.

"Maybe you need to get laid."

"Are you being funny?"

"Funny's when a small guy starts swinging his little dick."

Bruno came at him with a fist, but Jacob swept it aside and punched him on the jaw, then kicked him between the legs. And when he doubled over, kneed him in the head. The big guy went down like a sack of potatoes.

A guy came out the bar and saw him unconscious on the ground.

Jacob told him he was sleeping off the booze and walked away.

Saul and Josh were in a room having a private chat. Saul was drinking, while Josh was snorting. Saul told him, "Can't you lay off that shit?"

"It helps me think."

"You'd be brain dead without it."

"Man! You're worse than my fucking mother!"

"She should have slapped some sense into you. What did you find out?"

"It's not good. They're cops."

"The ones hitting the crooks?"

Josh snorted another line and nodded.

"Listen fucker, don't OD on me."

"I'm not the one you should be worried about."

"You mean the cops? Who are they?"

He told him their names. "Maybe we should cool it for a while."

Saul gave him a funny look. "You're bailing out on me?"

"Only till it blows over."

"Or maybe you'll get lucky, and I'll get dead?"

"Don't be like that, bro. How long have we been friends?"

"Too long," said Saul, bringing out a gun and shooting the dealer dead.

As Nancy stepped out of a diner, a car crept alongside her, and three guys started whistling.

"Hey, darling, fancy a lift?"

She told them to fuck off and carried on walking and heard footsteps behind her. When she turned around, something clubbed her on the head, and the guys were kicking and punching her on the ground. She woke up in a basement tied to a chair with the three guys standing over her.

She tried to make their faces through swollen eyes, but her vision was blurred. "I'm a cop. Let me go and I won't say nothing."

One guy smiled and told her, "The dead can't talk."

"They'll crucify you, if you hurt me."
"What do you care. You won't know."
"Fuck you!" she spat at them.
"No, baby, you're the one that's fucked."

They found the dead cop naked in a dumpster with her body mutilated. On her body were words painted in blood. "We reap what we sow."

The next day, Jacob walked into the precinct. Bruno was missing, and Nancy was dead. Matt looked like he had been drinking and hadn't slept. When Jacob tried to speak with him it was like talking to a stranger. The lieutenant pushed passed him and went outside. Harlan stopped Jacob at his car and asked if they could talk.

Matt went to the diner where Nancy was last seen and spoke to the owner. When he went outside, a car with three guys drew alongside him. One asked the time. Matt told them to get lost and made his way to his car that was parked next to an alley. As he went by the alley, he heard footsteps behind him and swung round with his gun.

The three guys froze with their hands in the air.

"Wow!" said a guy. "Take it easy, dude! What's with the heater?"

Matt told them, "I was just wondering which one of you murdered my partner?"

"Hey, we're not killers. Put it away."

"Wrong answer," said Matt, shooting him in the stomach.

Then turn to the one next to him. "Let's do this again."

"What's your problem, man!" cried the guy, stepping back.

"Wrong answer," said Matt, clinking the gun.

"Alright! Alright!" cried the guy, throwing out his hands. "Don't shoot! Don't shoot! What do you want to know?"

"Who murdered my partner?"

He pointed to his friend on the ground. "That guy!"

"Did she suffer?"

"Look, I just slap people around. I don't do the heavy stuff."

"You just slap them around."

"I'm like you. It's a job."

"You're nothing like me."

"We follow orders."

"And what did you do with the big guy?"

"What guy?"

Matt shot him in the chest. Then turned to the last one. "Let me rephrase that."

"Alright! Alright!" cried the guy, pointing to the guy he just shot. "It was him! He whacked your friend!"

"Everyone whacking everyone, except you."

"I'm just the muscle! I don't get into the rough stuff!"

"Yeah, you just watch. Who ordered the hit?"

"I don't know, man!"

Matt shot him in the leg.

"Alright! Alright! I'll tell you! But promise you won't kill me!"

"I just want the guy that set it in motion."

"It was a dude called Saul Goodman!"

"Where can I find him?"

After the guy talked, Matt shot him in the head. Then went looking for the cocksucker that killed his friends.

Harlan sat opposite Jacob and told him about their plot to take out the crooks.

"I wanted to do good," said Harlan. "Clean up the streets, but we started losing our way."

"But why kill them?"

"We only went after the killers. Courts are too soft on them. You put them away and some smart lawyer gets them out. Then they come after you for abusing their rights. The system doesn't work. So, we dispensed our own justice."

"And become a killer yourself."

"They got what they deserved."

"Is that what you told yourself when you slept at night?"

"We were making the world a better place."

"So, why are you coming clean now?"

"I saw myself becoming the people I hated. We crossed the line with Luke. I'm sorry. There was no excuse for what we did, and now I must make my peace with the Lord."

Harlan told Jacob how his brother died and the location of the body.

"Are you prepared to write everything down?"

"They say confession is good for the soul."

Jacob gave him a pen and paper.

Matt followed the gun runner's car. Saul parked by the side of a deserted road as if he was waiting for someone. There were three guys with him. He sat next to the driver, sharing a joke. Matt went to the car and tapped on the glass.

Saul's window came down. "Can I help you?"

"I'm looking for Saul."

"He isn't here."

"He looks like you."

"Do I know you?"

"Saul Goodman?"

"Is there a problem?"

"You killed my friends."

Saul stared at him like he couldn't believe what he was hearing, then turned to his guys and told them, "The balls on this guy."

When he turned back, there was a gun in his face. Matt shot him in his face. Then everybody started shooting.

Nancy, Bruno, Matt and Luke got a hero's funeral. There was no sense in shaming the department over something it had no control over, and the victims were criminals that the world wouldn't miss, except for an officer that died in the line of duty. His family would be compensated. Harlan retired early and was sworn to secrecy, which bought him immunity. If he broke the agreement, he would lose his pension and face jail time. The department was clean.

When Jacob went back to Brooklyn, he was sent on a job. Cops were surrounding a building where a cop was holding a hostage. He showed the officer in charge his badge and asked, what was going on?

The uniform pointed to a window. "There's a cop up there with a hostage asking for you. Are you a negotiator?"

"Do you know why?"

"I'm just here to secure the scene."

"Can I borrow your radio?"

The uniform gave him a funny look. "Haven't you got one?"

"Would I be asking?"

"Sorry, sir, it's in the car. Maybe if you ask around."

"Thanks for nothing."

"Anytime, Detective."

Jacob shook his head and raised a bullhorn, here we go again.

END

No Rest for the Wicked

It was the 1980s and the crack epidemic was taking over the streets of Miami. So, it needed a special kind of cop. Someone who could get dirty and play by their rules. The requirement of a cop was to be smart, resourceful and tough and there was no one tougher than Detective Lieutenant York. He was good cop. Good at his job, and the bad guys feared him because he talked with his gun and didn't tolerate fools, but his pursuit for justice often brought him bad press. Today, he was up before a disciplinary board, two men and a woman, for misconduct.

The man in the middle, who was the senior of the three, looked up from his notes. "Detective Lieutenant Raymond York, you have an unbelievable record. How it seemed to go unnoticed is beyond me."

"Just doing my job, sir."

"It wasn't a compliment. I see here you have a problem with authority and like to bend the rules."

"I get results."

"At the city's expense. It would be cheaper giving the crooks welfare than to send you after them. Are you trying to bankrupt the city?"

"I have a good arrest record. I'm out there every day, putting my neck on the line and saving lives. I should be getting a medal, not a reprimand."

"Your intentions may be noble, but we work as a team, and you're not a team player. It beats me how you ever became a lieutenant."

"I'm good at my job."

"Does that include excessive force?"

"When you're up against violent criminals. You apprehend them anyway you can."

"Well, this time you went too far. We have three bodies in the morgue and two of them are innocent victims."

The speaker conferred with his colleagues, then turned back to the detective.

"As of today, you're demoted to detective sergeant. What have you got to say about that?"

"You're punishing me for doing my job?"

"Keep it up and you'll soon be walking the beat."

"Try wearing a badge. You wouldn't last two minutes on the street."

"What was that, Detective?"

"Maybe you don't understand the concept of law enforcement."

"Are you being sarcastic?"

"It's easy to judge, when you're cozy at the top."

"That will be all, Detective."

York turned to leave. "Fucking politicians are worse than the crooks."

"What was that, Detective?"

York turned back to face them. "I said, have a nice day," he replied, and walked out the room.

The mayor received a phone call from his son's school enquiring if he was sick.

"Isn't he with you?" asked the mayor.

They told him that he had missed an exam. A little later, he got a call from a man claiming to have his son. At first, the mayor thought it was a hoax.

"How did you get this number?"

"How is unimportant. The only thing that should concern you is your son, Gabriel."

"Listen, sucker…"

"You can call me Phoenix."

The mayor was about to put down the phone when he heard his son's voice on the line. "Daddy! Daddy!"

He raised it back to his ear. "Gabriel, is that you?"

The man came back on the line. "Do I have your attention?"

"Who is this? What do you want?"

"$200,000 in unmarked bills."

"Are you crazy?"

"Do you want your boy back?"

"I don't have that kind of money."

"Then say goodbye."

"Alright! Alright!" cried the mayor. "When do you want it?"

"Call the police and your son dies. Are we clear?"

"I get it, no police."

"I'll call this number, same time tomorrow. Have the money ready and we'll do the exchange."

"Just don't harm my boy!"

"As long as you pay the money, he will be returned to you unharmed. Remember, have the money ready, and I want a cop called Raymond York to deliver the ransom."

"Why him?"

"Have him with you by the phone."

"I thought you said no cops?"

"Only him. Anymore and the boy dies. Are we clear?"

"I need more time."

"You have until tomorrow. Be ready."

"You do anything to him, and I'll hunt you down!"

"Do as I say, and he will not be harmed."

Before the mayor could respond, the line went dead. He looked at the receiver and sank to his knees.

Four men sat around a table playing cards. The man who called himself Phoenix was their boss. His brother was an ex-cop, now serving time, and needed money for protection. And he had York to thank for that.

Phoenix turned to the youngest member of the crew and told him to check on the boy, but Billy had a good hand, so he was reluctant to go.

"Boss, why don't you get someone else."

Phoenix told him, "How do you expect to get a cut if you won't work for it?"

"But why does it always have to be me?"

"We all have a part to play," said Phoenix. "Now be a good sport, and don't forget to wear a mask."

Billy, who was simpleminded, thought about the 20,000 Phoenix had promised him and left the room. The other two who were getting 50,000 a piece, smiled.

When Billy came back, Phoenix asked, "How is our guest?"

Billy told him, "Shaking like a rabbit. Are we going to let him go?"

"Why'd you think we wear masks," said Phoenix. "It's the cop we're after."

York walked into a restaurant and saw the mayor sitting alone at a table. He made his way over and sat opposite. "Why am I here?"

The mayor held out a hand. "Thank you for coming, Detective."

York ignored the hand. "I'm busy. So, let's get on with it."

"Have I done something to offend you?"

"I'll walk out if you don't tell me what you want."

"I need your help."

"Talk to my captain."

"I'd like to keep it between us."

"You got the wrong guy."

The mayor pushed a menu towards him. "Are you hungry, Detective?"

York ignored the menu. "This isn't a booty call, so let's skip the foreplay."

"Have you children, Detective?"

"You've seen my file."

"I have a 14-year-old son called Gabriel. Since my wife died, he's all I have. He was kidnapped this morning, and the kidnappers want you to deliver the ransom."

"Why me?"

"I was wondering the same thing."

"Maybe they have a beef."

"I understand you were demoted to sergeant. Help me and I'll get you your lieutenant shield back."

"You could do that?"

The mayor removed a photo of his son from his wallet and pushed it across the table to York.

"Bring him back alive and I'll be in your debt."

"What do they want?"

"$200,000 in unmarked bills."

"Did you get a name?"

"He called himself Phoenix and said no cops except you."

"And you want me to walk into a trap?"

"Put yourself in my shoes, Detective. He has my son."

York thought about it, and asked, "Fill me in on this Phoenix."

At 2 pm the phone rang. York picked up the receiver the same time as the mayor and listened on the extension.

"You have my money?" said the voice on the line.

"It's here," the mayor told Phoenix. "Now let me speak to my son."

"All in good time. Is York with you?"

"I'm here," said the detective. "How do you want to play this?"

The mayor interrupted them. "I want to know that my boy is still alive!"

"Daddy! Daddy!" cried a voice, then the man came back on the line.

"Okay, quit crying. Are you alone, York?"

"Nobody knows except us."

"Good. And you have 200,000 in unmarked bills?"

"Am I repeating myself?" said the mayor.

Phoenix laughed, "Stop bellyaching." Then told the detective, "Are you ready for an adventure, York?"

"Let's get this done."

"I like you, York. When this is over, maybe we could be friends."

"Where do you want the cash?"

"Don't go getting any wise ideas. Screw up and the boy dies. Got it?"

"Loud and clear," York told him.

"And no guns."

"I'm not packing."
"Good. Now pay attention…"
He was given a set of instructions.

As usual, the precinct was a hive of activity. The captain walked into the squad-room, and bellowed, "Where's York?"

The detectives looked at each other.

Patterson, who was the acting lieutenant, told the captain, "He's on loan to the mayor, sir."

"Doing what?"

Patterson shrugged. "Don't know, sir."

The captain looked around. "Who else knows?"

One hand came up, then another, and another.

The captain was furious. He arched a finger at Patterson and called him into his office.

Patterson stepped into the office and was told to close the door.

The captain gave him a hard look. "Run that by me again?"

Patterson looked at his shoes. "I thought you knew, sir."

The captain yelled at him, "York's a loose cannon, and I'm just hearing this now?"

"Whatever the mayor has him doing, I'm sure it's for the good of the city, sir."

"For how long?"

Patterson shrugged.

"Run that by me again?"

Patterson looked up, sheepishly. "No idea, sir."

"Did you ask?"

"It wasn't my business, sir."

"It wasn't your business!"

The captain shook with rage and pointed at the door. "Get out of my sight before I chain you to a desk!"

When Patterson was gone, he dialled a number and was put on hold. When he got through, a secretary told him that the mayor was in a meeting. "Would you like to leave a message?"

He slammed down the phone.

York was in a phone booth waiting for a call. An old lady tapped on the window and opened the door.

"Are you using it?"

York told her it was out of order.

"Why are you here?"

He showed her a badge and told her it was official business. "There's another box less than mile away." He pointed. "If you run, you'll make it."

She gave him a stubborn look. "Do I look like an Olympic runner!"

"Listen, lady, take it up with the department."

She shook her head. "I ought to report you to the real police!" And walked away.

The phone rang. He picked it up and spoke into the receiver, "Yeah?"

"Is that you, York?"

"Yeah."

"It's good to see my tax dollars at work," said Phoenix. "Are you ready for another trip."

"Your money's right here."

"All in good time. This is where I want you to go."

He was instructed to go to another box. So, he picked up the case and started running. When he got there, the phone was ringing. He snatched it off the hook. "Yeah!"

"You're late," said Phoenix.

"I'm not as fit as I used to be. Now stop fucking around."

"Are you giving the orders now?"

"Let's get this over with."

"Do you want the boy or not?"

"Tell me what to do."

He was given another set of instructions. When he stepped out of the box, two punks were waiting for him, with knives.

One of them pointed at the case. "That seems a little heavy."

He brought out a gun and told them, "Are we really going to do this!"

They looked at the gun, looked at each other, then back to the gun.

"Now get out of here before I change my mind!"

They were gone faster than Houdini.

When he got to the next box, it was ringing.

He snatched it off the hook, and shouted, "Yeah!"

"You're late again," said Phoenix.

"I was held up by a couple of punks."

Phoenix laughed. "You mean the punks outside?"

He turned around and looked through the glass and saw the same two goons waving guns at him.

When he stepped outside. They took the case, searched him, and found a gun and badge. Then they led him to a van, tied his hands, and made him sit in the back with a goon, while his partner drove.

The van stopped an hour later. The door opened, and Phoenix was standing there with a gun.

He pointed it at York. "Remember me?"

"Phoenix, right?"

"Do I remind you of someone?"

"How's your brother?"

"Better than you."

Phoenix showed him his gun. "You don't hear so well."

"I was protecting your money."

Phoenix smiled. "Well, no harm done."

"Now let the boy go."

"I'm a man of my word."

They brought him to a lonely house in the woods. When they walked through the door, Billy was in the lounge watching a *Tom & Jerry* cartoon on the telly.

Phoenix switched it off.

"Ah, boss!" cried Billy, "I was watching that!"

Phoenix told him it would rot his brain.

They took York to a basement and tied him to a chair. Then Phoenix left with his goons and locked the door.

York had expanded his chest and tensed his body when the rope went around him. Now he relaxed his muscles to make his body smaller, slackening the rope. He found a razor blade on his body, cut the rope, and wriggled free. Then he put the rope back around him to make it seem like he was still tied up.

When Phoenix walked into the room, the telly was on, and Billy was giggling at a cartoon. Phoenix told him to get the boy.

Billy came back with the kid. He had his hands tied behind his back and a hood on his head. When they put him in the back of the van, he smelled like he had soiled his pants. The goon that kept him company wanted to put a bullet in his head.

Patterson knocked on the captain's door and walked into his office. The captain was shaving in a mirror.

He stopped when he saw Patterson. "Who invited you in?"

"Sorry, sir, I have news on York."

"Well, spit it out!"

"The mayor's son was kidnapped. York is helping him with the ransom."

"Why wasn't I informed?"

"No idea, sir."

"When was he taken?"

Patterson shrugged.

The captain stuck his head out like an ostrich. "Well, what do you know?"

Patterson looked at his shoes. They needed a shine.

The captain gave him an incredulous look. "You're an idiot! What are you?"

Patterson kept looking at his shoes.

The captain threw up his hands and cried, "Why am I surrounded by incompetent fools!"

Billy unlocked the basement door and saw the detective bound to a chair. He had his eyes closed. So, he turned to leave.

"Hey!" cried the detective.

When Billy turned around, his eyes were open.

York looked disorientated. "How long have I been here?"

Billy told him a few hours.

"Where's the boy?"

Billy told him they were letting him go.

"So, you're on your own?"

"They'll be back soon."

"I'm thirsty. Can you get me some water."

"I'll get in trouble."

"Who's going to know? There's only us."
Billy scratched his head. "Gee, mister, I don't know."
"Please, it may be my last drink."
Billy hesitated.
"Please."
Billy thought about it and didn't see the harm. "Alright, I'll be back."

The cop was tied up. So, he left the door open and went away. When he came back with a glass, the chair was empty.

Surprised, Billy dropped the glass and went for his gun. But York came up behind him and put him to sleep with a headlock, then tied him up and took the gun.

The police received an anonymous tip and found Gabriel in an empty house. Drugged and bound. When questioned, he was vague about his abduction, the location, or the people behind it. He told them they wore masks.

The mayor held a press conference to quiet the speculation.

A reporter raised a hand. "Mayor, do you know the identity of the kidnappers?"

"It's unknown, but we're chasing some leads and confident of an arrest."

"What leads have you got?" asked another reporter.

"It's an ongoing investigation. I'm not at liberty to say."

He pointed to another reporter.

"How much was the ransom?"

"That confidential information is part of the investigation."

"Is a detective called Raymond York heading the investigation?"

"Yes, he's in the field now."

"Where is he?"

"Doing his job."

"Is it true that York is missing in action?"

"I don't know where you get your information."

"The same place you get yours!" cried another reporter.

There was laughter in the crowd.

One reporter turned to his colleague and told her, "What a crock of shit! He's an evasive, lying bastard, isn't he?"

Phoenix and the goons were jubilant as they got out of the van and made their way to the house. He was 200 grand richer. As they went to the door, Phoenix was whistling, 'Fly me to the moon'.

One goon said, "Did you hear that bastard on telly telling everyone they were going to catch us."

"Let him kid himself," Phoenix told them. "He's a politician."

"So, boss, what are you going to do with your share?"

"Worry about your own."

"What do we do about the cop?"

"I've got plans for that sucker."

The goon smiled. "I've always dreamt of doing a cop."

"Well good things come to those who wait."

As they went through the door, Phoenix was thinking about the Bahamas and beautiful girls. *Pussy, here I come.*

York was waiting for them with a gun on the other side.

York knocked on the captain's door and was told to enter. When he walked into the room, the captain was sitting behind his desk.

"You did good, Detective."

"Sorry I didn't keep you in the loop, sir."

The captain threw his lieutenant's shield on the table. "I believe congratulations are in order."

York put it in his pocket. "Sorry I forgot the wine. Do I get my old job back?"

"Your first task is to tell Patterson that his service is no longer required."

"Is that your way of saying you missed me, sir?"

"Don't let it go to your head."

The captain held out a hand. "Welcome back, Detective."

He shook it and left the room.

When York got to his office there was a mountain of paperwork. He put his feet on a table, laid back, and closed his eyes. *It will keep for another day.*

— *End* —

Customer Service

We pay taxes for everything, and no one wants to cheat the tax man, but it's crazy working with them. You ring them and wait half an hour on the phone to be told it's the wrong number. So, they give you a number for another department in the same building. It's the same number except for the last few digits. So, you ring the number and get a number for another department. The departments have different names, but they deal with the same thing. Your tax. I must have spent over two hours going through the different departments. It was frustrating. It was like they were passing me around because they didn't want to deal with my problem. I said to one guy, "The department is next door. Can't you get the information and process it? It's my information." But they have a bullshit system that prohibits them from doing any work. And the government claims that there's freedom of information. It's not free if you can't get it. I said to another guy, "I want to be honest and sort out my taxes, but the way you're treating me, I can see why people avoid you."

But the guy was on a government salary. He was probably thinking, *this is what I went to university for. I should have joined the army. At least when they fuck you, you can see it coming. Now I'm in debt for a fucking big loan.* He gave me another number.

People talk about money making you happy and end up hating their friends.

A guy was sitting under a tree with a bong. He'd lost his job, so he's crying to the wife, "What am I going to do?" She told him to get another job because bills need to be paid. So, he starts crying again. "That's all I'm good for! To pay the bills! Money doesn't grow on trees!"

So, she told him, "Well, you won't make it sitting under a tree smoking pot."

I met this bloke. He was bawling like a baby. So, I asked him what was wrong.

"My girl left me for missing a date."

"Your girl dumped you for missing a date. Man, that's cold."

He shook his head. "It was our wedding day."

Maybe you like rats. Well, here's a little something for you, rat lovers.

Who Needs Friends

Two rats are in a cage with high walls. So, one tells the other, "If I climb on your back, I can get over the wall."

"But what about me?" said the other rat.

"Don't worry, I'll be back with a ladder to get you out."

So, he gets on his back and goes over the wall. His friend's waiting for him to come back, but days go by, weeks, months, and he doesn't come back. So, now he's pacing around having suicide thoughts. Six months later, a note sails over the wall. It's a message from his friend with a smiley face: *Merry Christmas, sucker.*

The Mexican with the New Shoes

A Mexican looks in a shop window and sees some nice shoes. They're the finest shoes he's ever seen. So, he must have them, but they cost more than he could ever afford. So, he walks into the shop and offers to work for them, but the storekeeper tells him that he has all the help he needs.

But he's in love with the shoes. So, he falls on his knees and starts begging. So, the guy feels sorry for him and says he'll hold them.

"But it could take me forever!"

The guy tells him to take as long as he needs. So, he goes away and comes back a year later. The storekeeper still has the shoes. So, he gives him the money, and the guy goes to wrap them up, but the Mexican tells him to put them on his feet. He wants to show them off. So, he walks out the shop with his new shoes. The dude's a movie star, pushing people aside, crying, "Don't step on my new shoes!"

He's Moses parting the Red Sea. Al Pacino on heat. Moonwalking like Michael Jackson. "With these babies, I goanna get me a girl!"

He's so happy, he doesn't see the gringo in front of him.

"Hey, watch where you're going!" he yells.

The gringo stops to admire his shoes. "Nice shoes."

The Mexican smiles proudly and tells him they're alligator.

The gringo measures his foot against his shoes. "And about my size."

The Mexican laughs and tells him, "It's a pity you can't afford them."

So, the gringo brings out a gun and tells him to take them off.

The Mexican can't believe it! He's being robbed! So, he grabs his chest like he's having a heart attack, and cries, "Fuck no! You can't be serious!"

"Does it look like I'm joking? Either you take them off, or I'll remove them from your dead feet!"

The Mexican falls on his knees and starts begging, "Please, no, don't take my shoes! I work very hard for them!"

But the gringo waves the gun at him. "Your deal, amigo. You got until three."

He starts counting.

So, the Mexican takes off the shoes and throws them at him.

"I hope you die in them!"

The gringo smiles and leaves him his shoes. "Take it easy, sucker."

"Go fuck yourself!"

He waves and walks away.

—— *END* ——

You're probably thinking, *poor guy*. Well, there's a moral to the story. Don't walk around Mexico with new shoes.

And talking about crazy people. There was an election in Russia, but the self-appointed leader was the only candidate. His opponents kept having accidents. One fell off a tall building, another got killed in a jungle while on safari. But how he got there, no one knew. And another fell out of a plane without a parachute. The president's aide held a press conference to reassure people. "Those were innocent accidents."

The people knew it was bullshit but if they said anything, they'd get shot. So, they walked away and shook their heads. Just another day in Russia.

Four in the morning, guy in Russia is woken by a loud rumbling noise. He gets out of bed, looks out the window and sees Putin's tanks patrolling the street. He shakes his head "Every day it's the same shit!"

A disease was killing off poor people, so they asked the Tory government to do something about it. They brought out their cigars and threw a party. You think I'm joking! Maybe you were in a coma during lockdown.

A guy collapsed in the street and got taken to the hospital. A doctor examined his chest and said he had no heartbeat.

His colleague asked if he was dead.

"It's normal," the doctor told him. "He's a Tory."

Talking about politics, some bastards you can tolerate, but the Conservatives go too far. They gave Sunak a part in *The Wizard of Oz*. He played the Tin Man. "If I only had a heart."

A scorpion wanted to cross a river, but he couldn't swim. So, he asked a frog to take him over.

"But you will sting me," said the frog.

The scorpion laughed and told the frog, "Don't be silly. If I sting you, we will both drown."

So, the frog carried the scorpion on his back. Halfway across the river, the scorpion stung him. As they were drowning, the frog asked him, "Why did you do that? Now we will both die!"

So, the scorpion told him that he was a Tory.

Ever been to a party where the host thinks they're hotter than a movie star? This guy was on a roll boasting about how great he was and the dicks he sucked. People were sliding out the door until he had an audience of one. Himself.

Two boys are in a garden looking at two birds on a tree. One tells the other, "I bet the one on the left flies first."

"You're on," said his brother. "Tenner on the right."

Their dad comes out with a shotgun and shoots them both out of the tree, and cries, "There'll be no gambling in my house!"

Suckers Come and Go

Men keep their clothes forever, but women are always changing. I knew this bloke that got married in his 20s and when he died 40 years later, they buried him in the same suit. And another guy that lived for 80 years and only owned two suits in his life. One, when he got married, and the other when he was divorced. And don't get me started on the guy that walked around with a sleeping bag because his house was repossessed. He was married with a nice job, called the homeless suckers, and kept boasting about how it could never happen to him. Then one day he lost the job, and the wife left him. Well, guess what, sucker, isn't karma a bitch!

I once applied for a bank loan, so I could cover an investment. The bank guy asked, "Are you sure about this?" I told him to relax. I had a job for life. He took me aside and said, "There are only two things guaranteed in life. Death and taxes." I took out my pen and asked him where to sign. Six months later, I was unemployed.

Hi, folks, is it safe to come out? I bet you want to shoot me. Well, before you go crazy, let's hash this out like reasonable people. Look, buddy, it was only a suggestion. What's that, you want to burn my house with me in it? Well, fuck all that bullshit. While you're thinking about it, let me roll you a story…

Hits from the Bong

I remember getting stoned with my buddy. All day and night we'd be high. Fall asleep and start again. And folks would come round to chill.

"Hey, bro, don't get greedy with that bong."
"Relax, there's plenty to go round."
"That's mighty generous of you with my weed."
"Share and share alike. What's mine is yours."
"That's easy to say, when you haven't got anything."
"Hey, let me sprinkle some dust in it."
"What is it?"
"Angel dust."
"Go fuck yourself and get a brain transplant!"

And Cypress Hill would be playing in the background, and everyone would be rocking their heads. "We love you, Mary Jane…"

"Hey, dude, what time you got?"
"I don't know, but they're sending people to Mars."
"Have I been asleep that long?"
"Wait, let me ask Captain Kirk."

And roaches would be passed around, and we'd be smoking like monks in the Bahamas. It was a casual affair.

A brother's phone starts ringing. He answers his mobile. "Hi, baby… What's that… No baby, I'm broke… Yeah, I'll see what I can do… Yeah, later, dude."

As he's putting it away, one guy asks, "Was that your bitch again?"

He nods. "I should have married her mother. Moan! Moan! Moan!"

"What did she want?"

"Money."

The other guy shakes his head. "Leave that bullshit at home."

I know what you're thinking, *those suckers need a kick in the ass*, but it was cool smoking with my homeboys. It was a hassle-free zone.

End

I hate funerals. Standing around with a bunch of Grim Reapers pretending to be miserable and sad, but deep-down everyone's happy they're dead. And the wake after is just an excuse to get drunk.

"Hey, there's a free drink down the road. They're having a wake."

"How'd we get in?"

"Pretend you know him and look sad."

The last time I went to a funeral, they kicked me out for smoking weed.

"What's wrong with you? Haven't you any shame!"

I told them, "If you knew him, you'd be celebrating too."

And at the will reading, the guy told me, "Your father left you something."

"What is it?"

"His portrait."

"Hasn't he tortured me enough!"

That old bastard never got a Christmas card from me, but I was there at his funeral to make sure he was dead.

"Hey, Pastor, this isn't a joke?"

"Can't you see that he's dead."

"Can I hit him with a hammer to make sure?"

We didn't get on, but you shouldn't talk ill of the dead. "Anyone for champaign?"

The Joking Dead

Four guys and a medium are sitting round a table in a dark room doing a séance. They're holding hands, and she's shaking like she's having an orgasm.

One guy tells her, "Baby, if I knew you were this horny, I would have brought a friend."

The others start laughing.

She throws him a dirty look. *In your dreams, old man*, and starts shaking again. "I can feel it! I can feel it!"

"Keep it down, baby," said the guy next to her. "The others might get jealous."

More laughter.

"Quiet!" she tells him. "There's someone in the room!"

"Who is it?"

"He says, remember the snowy mountains!"

One guy joked, "Is that you, Pablo?"

And they start laughing again.

She tells them to hush. "He keeps saying, remember me... Remember me..."

"Who the fuck is he?"

She berates him for being rude. "There's another message... From your mother."

The four guys tell her that their mothers are still alive.

These old farts are nearly dead. So, she's thinking, *what are the odds?* She's fucked up and hopes they haven't noticed. "I have another message…"

"What is it?"

She tells them, "Be generous to the medium."

--- END ---

You're probably thinking, you can't get any nuttier than this guy. He needs a lobotomy. If we were in a jungle, I'd have eyes in the back of my head…

Guy wakes up in the jungle and sees his best friend sharpening a knife, watching him.

"Why are you staring at me like that?"

"I was just thinking if we don't get food soon, I may have to eat you."

"Yeah, well, fuck you! I'm jumping in the river!"

I'm no Hannibal Lecter but his legs would taste nice with some soya beans. I know, I have an outrageous sense of humour. What can I say, this bullshit comes naturally. My mother told me she dropped me on my head when I was a baby. I asked her why.

"You were crying too much."

I told her, "That's because I have a homicidal mother."

But seriously, she tried her best. It was just a bad time. Rest in peace, wherever you are. Now let's say a prayer for this bounty we're about to eat. "Oh, holy one, thank you for delivering me this sucker…"

"You crazy bastard! Untie me!"

The cab driver shakes his head. He's heard enough. "Is this bullshit going to take long? I'm on a meter!"

"Alright, stop here. My money's in that flat over there. I'll be back soon."

The cab driver stops the car, looks up at the tall building, and takes out his bat. "Look at me. Do I look like I was born on the stupid tree? I've got a bat here that thinks you should empty your pockets!"

"Don't you trust me?"

"I don't know you. Maybe we've met in a past life, but in this life, I'm going to bust your head if I don't get my money!"

"Hey, I'm joking. Got change for a 20?"

I get how social media is good for promoting your thoughts and ideas, but some people think they're superstars. They like to boast about how successful they are. "Look, I'm happy for you but I'm just an average Joe. I can't give you a medal." You see them in front of their big houses, flash cars, and boats, and they wonder how they got robbed. It's called advertising, suckers. You've invited the crooks into your homes. And they cry about the injustice. My heart goes out to you but don't dangle carrots in their faces. Then they tell you, "But everyone's doing it." If I jumped off a cliff, would you follow me? Don't answer that. I wouldn't want to put ideas in your head.

A man phoned the Good Samaritans, and cried, "I've got a gun and I'm going to kill myself!"

The guy on the other end, told him, "I'm putting you on hold. I'm taking another call."

Moaner Lisa

I was relaxing by the tele, having a munch, when my baby came into the room and started taking her off her clothes.

I told her she was putting me off my food. "Slow down, baby, I'm watching my favourite programme."

She pouted her lips and stamped her feet like a spoiled little child. "Don't you love me anymore?"

I told her now wasn't the time. "Now run along and play with that vibrator I got you for Christmas."

"You're turning me down for a fucking show!"

I told her it was *Suckers Got Talent*. "Now make yourself useful and get some tea."

She gave me an incredulous look. "I work hard, while you sit on your fat ass all day and do nothing, and this is the thanks I get! What did your last slave die of?"

"Baby, we'll play later."

"Who do you think you are?"

I wanted to say, *your worst nightmare*, but I just humoured her and smiled. "Is it your hormones again? Stop being a drama queen and I may even cook a meal."

"Well, don't do me any favours!" she told me, rushing to the door.

But I flew off the chair and wrapped my arms around her and showed her my adorable smile. "Baby, baby, what's wrong? Talk to daddy."

"I'm sick of this! I'm sick of you!"

"Has my baby had a bad day?"

She wriggled out of my arms. "Every day's a fucking bad day with you!"

I grabbed her back and gave her an affectionate squeeze. "Baby, baby, I'm sorry. How can I make it up to you?"

"My mother warned me about you!"

"Let me get you some tea and we'll talk about it."

"And you think tea is going to cut it?"

"It's a start, baby. What do you say?"

"Why should I?"

"Because I love you."

"Well, you have a funny way of showing it!"

"Let me get you that tea, so we can talk about it. And I have a present for you."

She looked suspicious. "Present?"

"Something I've been saving for a special occasion."

She crossed her arms and gave me a stubborn look. "You're a pig, you know that?"

"But I'm your little piggy," I cooed into her ear.

She shooed me away. "Well, go, before I change my mind."

Then she sat back and crossed those long slender legs.

Oh, how I despised her! The ruthless whore! As ruthless as the day was long!

So, off I went and came back with a steaming cup of brew.

"Here, baby."

She took it out of my hands and gave me a smug look. Then sipped it slowly and leisurely.

"So, what do you think?"

"I'll let you know after I get that present."

So off I went in search of my toy and when I came back, one could almost relish the look of horror on her face when she saw the thing in my hands.

I raised the chainsaw and pulled the cord, and the terrifying engine roared into life. "Did you miss me, baby?"

The cup fell out of her hands as she tried to flee, but her body wouldn't respond. Her arms and legs couldn't move. Paralysed, she looked down at the cup.

"That's right, baby," I told her. "It was drugged."

Her wild demented eyes were nearly popping out of her head. "Why?"

"So, I can cut of your legs, silly."

"You bastard! But why?"

So, I raised my jumper, brought out a book and dropped it on her lap like it was a hot potato. *Misery* by Stephen King.

---— END —---

Yeah, I know what you're thinking. *From now on, I'm making my own tea.* Well, here's some advice. Don't mess around with flowers. Get her a chainsaw instead. It will keep the relationship alive. But don't quote me on that. I'm on parole.

But seriously, I'm the last person you should go to for advice. Back in the early days, I was with a girl for six months, and everything was going great. Then one day we were in bed getting cozy and she asked if I would die for her. I told her she was with the wrong sucker. After that she went cold on me. I think we only lasted a week.

Once, a woman brought me to her flat. We're in bed sleeping, and something woke me. She was talking in tongues. It freaked me out! I shot out of bed fast and ran out the flat. For all I knew, she could be communicating with her demon friends. The next day, she phoned and asked if I was coming back. I told her to see a priest.

I was dating this woman. She kept finding fault with everything I said. So, I told her, "If there were stars in the sky and I said there were stars in the sky, you would disagree with me to spite me." But she wouldn't let it go. She slapped my face and told me I was rude. So, I said, "Alright, I'm sorry. You're right, and I'm wrong." But I got more grief for agreeing with her. So, I threw my hands in the air and told her, "You're like a monkey on my back, always riding me! When I'm right, I'm wrong! What can I do to keep the peace?" She started pissing and moaning some more. So, I thought, *fuck it! I'm out of here! I'm done with this bullshit!* "You're on your own!"

In the winter you'll see me walking around in the freezing cold in just a T-shirt and shorts. It's invigorating. I love the fresh air. It could be below zero and I'll have all the windows open in my flat. Once, a friend came round and said it was like the North Pole. I told him to wear gloves and a better coat. I had a girl over for some nookie, but it was too cold to do anything. Before she left, she told me, "Good luck with the next one."

Some guys get off on dominating women and keeping them on a chain. You can't do this, and you can't do that. Listen, ladies, don't put up with that bullshit. Tell him,

"If I want to go out in just my panties and bra, you're driving."

These are freer times. I like how women have got the freedom to do whatever they want. And they're having such a great time doing it, guys are converting to the other side. "Is that you, Harry?"
"People call me Sally now."

Remember being young and in love. It's a romantic night. Guy steps out of a club with a beautiful girl and thinks he's pulled. He gets her a cab and asks, "Will I see you again?"
She points at the sky. "You see that star up there."
He smiles dreamingly and nods.
"You'll have more luck getting a rocket to it."

Two old ladies are gossiping about a couple on the street.
"You see that guy over there. He's 33, married with three kids."
"That's young, but why does he look so old?"
"He has a demanding wife."

We get judged by how we look and told what is acceptable behaviour, but what is acceptable behaviour? There used to be a time when sex out of wedlock was an unforgivable sin. Horny people were sent to doctors and priests to get their heads examined, but now we live in a promiscuous society, everyone's at it. Some, with more than one partner. And if you're not doing it, there must be something wrong with you. Go figure.

Some guys can't take rejection. It offends their pride. Well, we live in a new age of sexual enlightenment and people dress up and use toys. So, if you get lonely, you can borrow my doll, Cindy. She has big boobs and a nice bum. Maybe in a few years they'll make an AI to replace your partner. "Hi, I'm Cindy, and I go both ways." But until then, use your imagination.

My Brush with the Black Widow

Ever been on a blind date? My friend fixed me up with a woman who had just lost her husband in an accident. So, I'm getting ready for the date, but feel guilty, and bottle out. She took it the wrong way and started badmouthing me to her friends. The way they looked at me on the street you'd have thought I had killed him. My heart goes out to a grieving widow but going out with a guy the same week you've buried your husband seems a little cold. Maybe they should reopen his case...

"Lady, the autopsy came back, and your husband was murdered."
"Alright, I confess."
"Why did you do it?"
"He was no good in bed."
I had a narrow escape.

"Quick! Open the door! Here comes that famous guy!"
"Did we lay out the red carpet?"
"Check!"
"Do you think he likes sushi?"
"And don't forget the champaign!"
"Is everything ready?"
"We'll make it ready! The guy's a VIP!"
"What about his book?"
"Shit! I knew there was something we forgot!"

"I'll stall him while you get it!"

"You want me to find a bookstore at this time of night?"

"Smash a window if you have to but bring me his book!"

"Okay, okay, but there's just one problem."

"What's that?"

"I don't know his name."

Guy tells another guy, "Want to see something funny?"

The guy asked, "What?"

So, he gave him a mirror.

Living in America

When I was a kid, I remember seeing a movie about life on the streets of New York. Two friends were having a disagreement in a bar. So, one guy pushes the other and says, "Let's dance, fucker!" I thought they were going to waltz, but it was like the O.K. Corral. Tables and chairs went flying and everyone got involved. It was a free-for-all. One old lady hit a guy with a bottle, and another guy punched her over a table. Just another night in an American bar. The Yanks are crazy. They think assaulting people is funny.

Around the Civil War in the South when they were having all that trouble with slavery, the Ku Klux Klan would be lynching Black people while white families would be picnicking. It was family entertainment. They even sold postcards. Little Billy would read one before he went to school. Even the preacher was in on it. Telling them, "Black people are an abomination on our country. It's our Christian duty to torture them. And I'm selling hoods if anyone's lynching. The money will go to a good cause."

Yeah, the Devil's cause. You evil bastards! They were so deluded. They thought they were doing God's work. "Welcome to white Heaven." Maybe now while they're roasting in Hell, they'll think about the error of their ways. Merry Christmas, you Nazi fuckers!

Anyway, imagine an English guy visiting New York with his family. He walks through a bar and knocks over some dude's drink.

The dude is pissed. "Hey, watch where you're going!"

The English guy tries to apologize, but the American can't hear him. There's loud music in the background.

"What was that? I'm a damn fool?"

The English guy shouts, "No! I said, I'm sorry!"

But the American still can't hear him. "What was that? My mother's a whore?"

The English guy tries to calm him down and takes out his wallet. "Let me get you another drink!"

The American rubs his chin. "Wait! Where have I heard that accent before? You're British?"

The English guy smiles. "You Yanks catch on fast! No wonder you won the war!"

The American dude laughs and slaps his back. "Hey, brother, put it away. This one's on me!"

---— END —---

You get the far-right protesting for a white England, when we live in a muti-cultural country with different nationalities. Someone ought to remind them it isn't the '70s anymore with the National Front. Look around, there are mixed families everywhere. That pure white bullshit is nonsense. I bet it's in your genes. Check with your doctor. There may be some Black inside you.

"Doctor! Doctor! I keep dreaming that I'm Black!"

"That's because you're a brother. Chill out and have a joint."

In the next story, we all like to please our mothers, but this guy's taking it a little too far. They say crazy runs in the family. Well, let's hope it isn't contagious.

Mother's Day

My friend Billy sat at the table eating a meal that my mother had lovely prepared for him. I had tricked him into accepting her kind invitation, and now that he was partway through it. He was like a condemned man. There was misery and regret in his eyes.

Mother sat opposite him, eager for approval. "How is the food, Billy?"

Billy was too polite to lie. So, he smiled and avoided her eyes. "It's fine, Mrs Reaper. Thank you."

Mother smiled sweetly at him. "Would you like more, Billy?"

He nearly choked and looked at his watch. "Oh, damn! I'm going to be late for an appointment!"

"What appointment?" I asked him.

"It's work! Look, I better go!"

"But you've only just got here."

"It's an important meeting!" he stuttered.

"Mother went to a lot of trouble for you. The least you could do is finish your meal."

He threw daggers at me with his eyes. Then turned to Mother. "Mrs Reaper, please accept my apology. We'll do this again later."

I told him he was hurting mother's feelings, and he was being rude.

"And why bother to come, if you had somewhere else to be?"

"I thought maybe... I thought maybe..."

"Yeah, you thought you could insult my mother and leave!"

"Alright, alright, I'll stay another 15 minutes, then I really must go!"

He went back to his meal like a trapped animal. Stabbing the plate with his fork. I could almost feel it going into me.

"Couldn't you just die," I told my used-to-be friend.

"What do you mean?" he asked with trembling lips.

I pointed at his plate. "People would die for that." And joked, "And people would die because of it."

With those light-humoured words, I had severed our friendship, but what did I care. Just watching him made it all worthwhile. It seemed as if that was the final insult as he threw down his cutlery and openly cursed me! Then he doubled over in pain and rolled off the chair.

As he convulsed on the floor, I told him, "Want to know the ingredients?"

But my words fell on deaf ears as he rolled around crying and moaning.

I told the sucker, poison. Then turned to Mother and saw her dancing around like a little girl, wetting her pants with all the excitement. It seemed such a pity to spoil her fun.

"Come on mother," I told her. "It's time for your medication."

End

Hi, folks, the man you love to hate is back! Wait a minute, did I get that right? Anyway, I've got some goodies that will put a smile on your face. Next up is a tale about two crooks digging a grave.

"Before you put me in the ground, can I have a smoke?"

"Hurry up, Mr Bond, time is ticking."

It's called...

More Money for Me

Two hired killers are digging a grave. When it's deep enough, they look for the body but can't find it. So, one guy tells the other to look in the car. He comes back and tells him it's not there. So, the first guy shakes his head. "Where the fuck is it?"

His partner scratches his chin. "I thought you, had it?"

"Do you see a body in my pocket?"

"Well, I didn't lose it."

"Then whose fault, is it?"

"We both fucked up, alright!"

The first crook calms down and holds up a hand. "Alright, alright, but we still have a problem. We need the body."

"He's dead, so what's the problem?"

"We need the body in a grave to get paid."

"Won't they hear about it on the news?"

"No, we have to go back for it."

"Fuck them! Let's get our money and get out of here!"

"We need to take a picture of the body in a grave to get paid."

His partner shakes his head. "There could be cops crawling all over the place!"

"We have to honour the contract."

"So, you're saying we need a body and a grave?"
"Those are the rules."
"But what if it's messed up and they can't recognize it?"
"It's the nature of the job. They'll take it on faith."

The second crook thinks about it, then points at something in the grave. "Did that fall out of your pocket?"

His partner bends down to look and gets whacked on the head with a shovel and thrown in the grave. Then the second guy starts shooting him.

— END —

I know, who need friends, but as they say killing is a ruthless business and there's no honour among thieves. "Now has anyone seen my camera?"

The Trigger-happy Hood

Six guys are in a room. Four hoods, their boss, and a prisoner. The prisoner's tied to a chair being interrogated. The boss is asking the questions:
"Look, I know you did it. I just want to know how."
The prisoner hangs his head and stares at the floor.
"Tell me what I want to know, and I'll go easy on you."
The guy acts dumb.
"Hey, dumb ass, don't I even get a nod?"
But the prisoner acts like he doesn't know nothing.
"So, that's how you want to play it."
Behind the boss, a hood is slapping his hand with a cosh.
"Want me to soften him up, boss?"
But the boss tells him no. "I'll call you when I need you, Rocky."
But Rocky wants to try out his cosh. He hasn't christened it yet. "Move aside, boss, I'll make him talk."
But the boss pulls him back and looks at Rocky like he's a child. "Did you fall on your head when you were a baby?"
But Rocky's eager for some action. He pulls out a gun and points it at the prisoner. "Just give me a minute with him, boss! I'll have him singing like a canary!"
The boss takes it off him. "Are you crazy? Cool down with some lemonade!"

But Rocky wants to slap the prisoner. "He's laughing at you, boss! Let me handle it!"

The boss slaps his face. "What's wrong with you? You don't hear so good!"

"But boss, he's laughing at you!"

"I give the orders around here, not you!"

Rocky starts moaning. "Come on, boss! Let me show you what I can do!"

The boss shakes his head. He's got no time for fools and tells his goons to restrain him. So, they grab Rocky and wrestle him to the floor.

Rocky goes down yelling, "But I'm doing it for you, boss!"

Boss tells him, "You're too eager to whack somebody. Next time it might be me."

"I could never do that, boss!"

"That's because you won't get the chance. One day you may get trigger-happy and turn that finger on me."

"What are you saying?"

Boss tells his goons to take Rocky and drop him off a tall building. So, they beat Rocky with their guns and drag him away.

A goon picks up Rocky's keys and asks if he could have his wheels.

Boss waves him away. "And bring me his eyes as a memento."

Then he turns to the prisoner. "If I can do that to one of my guys, imagine what I can do to you."

The prisoner starts jabbering like he has verbal diarrhoea.

— End —

"Cops rounded up some crooks. Half of them were politicians."

His friend shakes his head. "So, tell me something I don't know."

Four cops robbed a shipment of drugs. When they sold the drugs, the boss told them to sit on the money, so they won't bring attention to themselves. One cop bought a house, another a boat, and another, a Ferrari. He's driving it around like he's Stirling Moss. The boss is furious and tells them they're looking to get caught. So, one guy told him to relax. They have the chief of police in their pocket. It was his shipment.

Three hoods are sitting round a table, planning a job. The boss gives them instructions and asks, "Any questions?"

A crook puts his hand up and tells him, "Yeah."

"What's that?"

"We're in the sky, robbing a plane. How do we escape?"

Mastermind rounds up a gang of villains and tells them, "We're going to pull a robbery and film it on live TV."

One crook gets up to leave and tells him, "Good luck with that."

Crooks have just pulled off a job. One crook tells the boss, "You've got an army of us hitting a drug warehouse with rocket launchers, armoured cars, and a speed boat. We make off with twenty grand, and four kilos. You've spent more money than you've made. So, I got to ask you a question."

"What's that?" asked the boss.

"Are you new at this?"

City of New York, bank's being robbed, alarms are going crazy! Bandits are running in and out with the loot. One guy sees another guy watching, and asks, "What's going on?"

"Can't you see? The bank is being robbed."

"But where are the cops?"

So, the man looked at him as if he was stupid and told him, "They are the cops."

Guy robbing a bank gets cornered by the cops. They're waiting outside, so he cries, "Hey, cops, if I come out with my hands up, you won't shoot?"

They cry back, "We won't shoot!"

So, he goes out with his hands up. 'Bang! Bang! Bang!'

"Hey, where's that guy that's going to save us?"

"You mean Van Damme? The guy telling everyone he's a hero?"

"Yeah, him."

"He had to run. Said it was an emergency."

The guy looks around like he's losing his shit. "Tell everyone they're going to die!"

A man talks to his girlfriend on his computer and tells her, "Listen, baby, I've got a confession. I'm an informer for the FBI and the Mafia are looking for me."

They're interrupted by a hacker's voice. "That's good to know." And see his face and street on the screen.

The guy starts yelling, "Shit! We're on live TV!"

A couple had a child and called him Joker. Every time Joker went to school, the other kids would laugh at him. One kid told him, "Hey, Joker, your parents must have a sense of humour for giving you that name."

He told them, "Not anymore. I've just killed them."

Three guys lost their money on the stock market. So, they made a pact to commit suicide. They're standing on the roof of a tall building, daring each other to jump, and decide to draw straws. The shortest goes first. So, the one with the short straw tells his buddies goodbye and jumps. When he's gone, one guy says to the other, "I forgot to tell him that he just won the lottery."

Cowboys and Gangsters

North America, 1826, three cowboys discover a spaceship and find a time machine on it. They mess around with it and get transported to 1936.

They appear in front of some hoods. The gangsters train their guns on them.

The boss steps between them. "Hey, where did you guys come from?"

The cowboys look around.

"Has the cat got your tongue?"

"Where are we?"

The Italian boss laughs, and tells his guys, "We're in the middle of New York and these clowns want to know where we are!"

They're disorientated and confused.

"Did the Irish send you?"

The cowboys are apprehensive and scared. They see tall buildings, machines on wheels, people bustling around, and hear crazy noises!

Boss snaps his fingers in front of their faces. "Is anybody at home?"

They wonder if they're in Hell. "Are we dead?"

The boss laughs.

One hood tells the boss, "Want me to finish them?"

But the boss holds up a hand. "These guys amuse me. Let's play along."

He turns to the cowboys. "I'll ask you one more time. Did the Irish send you?"

But the cowboys are lost and confused.

Boss looks at their faces to see if it's an act. "Did you boys fall out of the sky? And what's with the rags?"

They look at him like they don't understand.

"The funny costumes?"

They still don't understand. So, he takes out a cigar and studies them.

"You guys really don't know where you are."

The cowboys look around, trying to make sense of it all.

Boss tells them, "Maybe someone should put you out of your misery."

"What is this place?" said a cowboy.

"Where do you think it is?"

"Are we in Hell?"

Boss laughs. "Would you like to be?"

But their eyes are wandering around.

So, he clicks his fingers to get their attention. "Hey, snap out of it!"

Then takes a step back and shakes his head.

"What shall we do with them, boss?"

"Dig a hole and make these guys comfortable."

"Gladly, boss!"

They beat the cowboys with their guns and drag them away.

---— END —---

Man, I'm glad I haven't got a time machine. I'd probably end up in the Deep South before Abraham Lincoln's time.

"Excuse me, is there a Black bar around here?"
"You've come to the KKK cleansing party."
"Sorry, guys, wrong place."
They put on their white hoods and start smiling. "You can say that again."

Law of the Jungle

It's a nice day, Joe's walking through the jungle like it's the Garden of Eden. He sees two monkeys on a tree and waves. They've seen him around. He's a nice guy. So, they smile and wave back. Joe carries on walking and comes across a posse of elephants. They wag their tails and Joe pats a few backs and carries on walking. Further along he sees a lion, a tiger, and their cubs licking some bones. So, Joe asks what was on the menu. They tell him a couple of hunters. "For slaying our brothers and sisters."

Joe tells them, "Right on," and carries on walking.

As he's walking through some trees, a bear steps in his path and tells him to take another route. So, Joe asks, "Why?" The bear told him a couple of trees have fallen, and the hyenas were clearing a path.

So, Joe goes another way. As he's coming to the end of the jungle, an alligator leaps out of a bush and stops him from leaving. So, Joe asks, "What's up?"

The alligator told him, "You're a nice guy, Joe, and everyone likes you, so I've got to ask you a question before I eat you."

Joe asks, "What's that?"

"Do you believe in God?"

— END —

No offense to all you animal lovers.
When you're eating that steak
remember where it came from.

What's a Little Murder Between Friends

Ross was sitting on a park bench, drinking lager from a can, when a stranger asked if he could sit beside him.

Ross told him, "As long as you're not gay."

"Are you homophobic?" asked the stranger.

"I've got nothing against gays as long as they keep to their side of the fence."

"They ought to lock you up and throw away the key."

"Why, are you gay?"

"I like girls, but I say live and let live."

"Well, good luck with that attitude."

The stranger asked if he had women trouble.

"The worst kind. Anyway, what's it to you?"

"Looks like we're in the same boat."

"I'll make a deal with you," said Ross. "You tell me yours and I'll tell you mine."

"And whoever tells the best story, gets free drinks in the pub."

"You're on," said Ross. "You can do the honours."

"I'll let you have the privilege."

So, Ross told his story...

"Been living with this girl for six months. One day she gets bored with straight sex and wants to go kinky. So, she talks about having a threesome with some guy from work. I told her to fuck off. So, we argue, make up, and get drunk. So, I wake up the next morning and go to work. My boss calls me into her office and shows me a film on her computer. It's a porno with me and some poof. We're naked and he's shagging my ass. I couldn't believe it! I thought they were fucking with me. Then it hit me. The bitch drugged the booze and while I was sleeping, set me up with the poof. Then sent the pictures to my boss to make me look like a pervert. I didn't know where to hide my face! I shot out of there fast!"

"Why did she do it?"

"Fuck knows! Couse she's a psycho bitch!"

"What happened to your job?"

"I might lose it."

"What do you do?"

"I'm a teacher."

The stranger laughed. "Can't you get the cops involved?"

"And get plastered on the six o'clock news? Be real."

The stranger was pissing himself laughing.

"So, what happened to you?"

"You think that's bad, well listen to this."

So, the stranger told his story…

"Met a bird in a club. We did some coke, I took her home, and she stayed at my place for a while. One day, she tells me to hook her up with my cousin who's a dealer. So, I ask her what's wrong with your guy? He got caught. So, I take her to my cousin and we're doing the deal when the door crashes open and the cops come in. They find a couple of kilos of coke. So, they take us to a station and put us in separate cells, and guess who we see walking around in a uniform. My bird. She's a cop. So, my cousin puts two and two together and thinks I'm a grass!"

"Come on, you must have known."

"The bitch was good! I was fucking her!"

Ross shakes his head. "She fucked you to get to your cousin?"

"Fucking unbelievable!"

"You should sue the cops."

"I would if I had money. And now I've got his mates after me."

"And I thought my troubles were bad."

"I guess, you're buying."

Ross took a drink from his can and offered it to the stranger.

The stranger gave him back the can and brought out a joint. "Those bitches really did us over."

"That O.J. Simpson had the right idea. I'd like to keep his glove as a souvenir."

The stranger lit up and took a hit from the joint. "Wouldn't you like to get even?"

"What could we do?"

The stranger passed the joint to Ross. "I'll kill yours, if you kill mine."

Ross nearly choked on the joint. "You're joking, right?"

"Do you see me laughing."

"We'll never get away with it."

"We would if we both had alibis."

Ross looked at the stranger to see if he was serious. "You're fucking with me?"

The stranger held his eyes. "We'll do it at different times and be miles apart. Then we go our separate ways."

"But do you really think it would work?" said Ross, passing back the joint.

"If we never see each other again."

Ross rubbed his chin and thought about it. Crazier things have happened.

"So, what do you say, partner?" said the stranger, holding out a hand.

Ross looked at the hand, then shook it. "Well, what's a little murder between friends."

End

Licence to Steal

The cops think they're clever. One way of getting rid of a complaint is to provoke the victim. The poor guy's already gone through the bullshit of getting robbed, and now they're giving him a hard time. So, he shouts at the phone and is told to calm down. "Lower your voice, sir. We can't help you if you're angry."

But the victim knows they're taking the piss. "You think this is angry! Well, fuck you!" and slams down the phone.

The cops are in a bar with a few villains, laughing at the recording. One crook tells him to play it again and they're wetting themselves, laughing.

"So, are you going to help him?" asks a crook.

"And waste valuable drinking time?" said a cop, and they start laughing again.

I know what some of you honest citizens are thinking: *oh, no, our cops can't be like that?* Well, good luck with that attitude.

When I was a kid, kung fu was the craze, and everyone wanted to be like Bruce Lee. People would throw a few moves and dance in the air. And some of them were good. Then one day I saw two guys having an argument. One bloke started kicking and punching the air. I was impressed. I thought he was Jackie Chan.

All that fancy stuff looked good on paper until the other bloke walked over and knocked him out with one punch. I went away thinking, *maybe I should be like Rocky.*

Pimping Ain't Easy

Friday night, two Black dudes get together in a bar and talk about their girls. They're sitting at a table, drinking tequila and smoking joints. And Marvin Gaye's 'Heard it Through the Grapevine' is playing in the background.

One pimp tells the other, "Every day's a headache with these girls. It's like running a zoo. There's one trick that has a smack habit, but she's a friend of a friend, so I let it slide, but she's breaking my balls."

"What's the pussy like?" asks his friend.

"Vanilla ice cream."

"Well, lay it on me."

"You'd be balling her instead of making money."

His friend laughs. "So, what's she like?"

"She's a good worker and the johns like her, but she's fucked up."

The other pimp rubbed his chin. "And you get to service the pussy."

"Got to sample the goods."

His friend smiled. "Well, wear a rubber."

"With my dong, I need a sock."

They both start laughing. Then he tells him a story.

"It's a slow day. She's working the street and needs a fix. So, she does a john in an alley, then goes to a bar and calls her dealer. She orders a drink while she's waiting and gives the bar guy the john's money.

He checks the bills and sees that they're fake and calls the cops, and they send over a couple of suits. It's colder than Moscow on the fourth of July and they're wearing sunglasses like fucking spies."

"And they didn't get made?"

"Her mind's someplace else. So, the dealer comes in and takes her to the toilet. They're doing it in a stall when the suits kick open the door and find her sucking his dick."

The brother is holding his chest, laughing. "Shit! So, what happened?"

"They take them to the station and put them in separate cells. The dealer's yelling for a lawyer and the bitch is screaming for a fix. She tells them if she doesn't see a doctor, she may soon need a priest. They tell her that her doctor's a drug dealer and he's going away for a very long time, and she may join him if she doesn't talk."

The brother shakes his head. "So, did she talk?"

"My girls are dumb, not stupid. She's screaming for a fix, and they don't want to find her dead in the cell. So, they cut her loose."

The brother can't stop laughing. "All this on account of the joker with the fake bills."

"That sucker better have somewhere to hide."

"Don't your girls go to school?"

"They haven't got the sense to learn."

The brother rolls a joint. "So, what's the deal with the credit cards?"

"The johns were getting robbed, and it was bad for business. This way, they don't handle cash, and we get a record of what they spend."

"Don't the cops give you a hard time?"

"They get their cut and everyone's happy."

"And a piece of the pussy."

The brother shakes his head. "These days it's hard to tell who the crooks are."

"Look for a badge."

The cats are laughing.

"Man, you play a tight game."

"And every game has its players."

The brother held out a palm. "Well, I dig your style."

The dude slapped it. "Right on," and passed him the joint.

--- *END* ---

These sex traffickers will steal anything off the street. In the sex business anything sells. You leave your grandmother outside a supermarket, come out and she's gone. A few weeks later, you see her on a sex site as a dominatrix. You scroll back and think, *wait a minute!*

Valentino's Big Break

Porn star Rudolph Valentino is in the film studio getting ready for a scene. The director tells him that the woman he was acting with couldn't make it, but there's another part he could play. He asks, "What is it?" They tell him it's a gay scene with another guy.

Rudolph's shocked. It would tarnish his reputation with the women. So, he tells the director to find someone else.

The director asks if he's homophobic.

He tells the director that he has nothing against gays, but he's a pussy kind of guy.

"So, you're a pussy guy?"

"I only do chicks."

"Well, listen, hotshot, while you're drilling his ass, pretend it's a pussy."

"I don't do guys."

"That's the job."

"Then get some other sucker."

"Well, let me go tell the boss. He doesn't like homophobic people. Pack your stuff. You're finished in this business."

Rudolph stops him. "Wait a minute! Can't we just stroke our dicks?"

"That's what the audience are for."

"Even the straight guys?"

"When they see your dick, they'll forget they were straight. Look, I like you, but if you turn it down, I've got to tell the boss, and the boss doesn't like homophobic people. So, what's it going to be?"

He thinks about it and asks, "How long is the movie?" The director tells him two hours.

"I've got to fuck him for two hours?"

"And suck dick."

The great lover is shocked. He tells the director, "I didn't sign up for this! Get somebody else!"

The director shrugs and turns away. "Alright, good luck with your next job. Don't forget to put porn star on your job application."

But Rudolph stops him from leaving. "Alright! Alright! But there better be a shit load of money!"

"Relax," said the director, "you'll be well paid. Just keep your dick up." He looks at his watch. "Well, better start rolling. Rub some oil on it before you get on the set."

And as he's walking away, remembers something and comes back. "Oh, and there's another gig tomorrow."

"What is it?"

"Have you ever done a donkey?"

The porn star can't believe what he's hearing! "Are you fucking with me?"

"Don't shoot the messenger. You want me to say that to the boss?"

"Queer fucking where I draw the line!"

The director tells him it's five figures.

So, he rubs his chin and thinks about it, and asks, "How high will he go?"

END

Guy sitting in front of a computer with his girlfriend. He's got his dick out, scrolling through a sex site and sees a woman in a wig playing with a dildo. She looks familiar.

His girlfriend puts on her glasses. "Hey, Frank, isn't that your mother?"

He takes a closer look and loses the erection.

Hey, I'm kidding! What you do in your own home is your business. Just don't forget to sell me a ticket.

Some people will do anything to get in the movies. A guy auditions for a movie. They get him to fuck a chicken and tell him he's got the part. He's ecstatic. "Great! When do I start?"

They tell him, "Don't worry, we've got you on film."

There was a family man married to a woman. Just an ordinary, everyday guy. Then one day he walked into the house with a Mohican haircut.

The wife was shocked. "What have you done?"

He told her he had just watched a Robert De Niro movie, *Taxi Driver*, and it had inspired him.

"Well, the children will freak out!"

He shrugged, "Let them. So, what do you think?"

She told him she wasn't ready for any more children and asked for a divorce.

The Brother in the New Suit

A brother's wearing a new suit because he's going on a date. He's seen her picture but hasn't met her. So, he walks into a bar and sees the girl sitting at a table. It's love at first sight. He strolls over and sits at the table. They both say hi.

She tells him, "You do know this is a casual date and it's summer?"

"I wanted to look good for you."

"Well, t-shirt and jeans would have done."

"Next time I'll bring my surfboard."

She laughs. "So, it's for me?"

"Baby, everything is for you."

"So, you want to impress me?"

"Baby, I'll do anything for you."

"Well, I hope you like kids?"

"You want kids?"

"I have four."

He stares at her uncomprehendingly, too stunned for words.

"I thought you knew?"

He gets up to leave and tells her, "It was nice knowing you."

Brother John

It was the night of the Drug Anonymous meeting. They met once a week to talk about their addiction and offer each other support. It was a small group, seven men and four women, including the group leader who was an ex-addict. The atmosphere was congenial, and everyone was in a friendly and loving mood.

The first speaker, a woman, had just finished her story, and it went round to the next person. Jeff had been a heroin addict since he was a child and was struggling with his addiction. He talked about his difficult week, and how he fought against the temptation to use. The group clapped and offered words of encouragement, then it went onto the next guy, John, who was new to the group.

The group leader introduced him. "This is John and he's a new member. So, let's welcome him to the group."

Everyone greeted him. The group leader gave him a warm smile. "Coming here was brave, John. Why don't you tell us about your addiction."

John looked at his shoes, too shy to talk.

"It's alright, John, we were new too. It takes a little getting used too. You can talk freely, and no one will judge you. What you say here will not go beyond these walls. This is a circle of trust. We are all friends. So, what do you say?"

John shook his head, reluctant to join in.

So, the group leader gave him a sympathetic look. "Coming here was hard, John, but it was the right thing to do. Now you need to talk about it."

John told them he wasn't ready.

The group leader smiled. "Do you work, John?"

John nodded.

"That's good. Work can be a distraction from our addiction, and it's a means of support, but it's difficult if we try to fight it alone. What do you do?"

John continued looking at his shoes.

"Is it honest work?"

John nodded.

"Then there's nothing to be ashamed of. You're making an honest living and that's all that matters. So why don't you share it with us?"

John shook his head.

"John, sharing enables us to build trust in this group. We are all in the same boat. There is nothing you could say that will embarrass you. I ask because it would help us understand how you live your life. Can you share that with us?"

John looked up from his shoes. "Do you really want to know?"

The group leader gave him an encouraging smile. "We're your friends, John, and we want to help you."

So, John gave them all a guilty smile and told them, "I'm a cop."

— END —

Have-a-go Charlie

I knew this bloke. Sober, he was one of the nicest people you could meet, but drunk, he was Jekyll and Hyde. I went pubbing with him a few times, but he got me into trouble. He'd eyeball people, and they'd look back wondering what was going on. And he'd tell them, "What are you staring at?"

"I'm just having a quiet drink with my girl."

"Well, you chose the wrong pub." And he'd start smacking the geezer.

It was mental. People would avoid him. Even the pub landlord was wary. I kept out of his way to have an easy life. Friends would stop me on the street and say he was looking for me.

"Where is he?"

"In the pub."

"Tell him I'll see him later."

I broke away from that crowd. The last time I saw him I was going to his funeral.

When the Going gets Tough

Laurel and Hardy have fallen on hard times, so they rob a bank. As they come running out with the loot, a cop car comes speeding towards them. Hardy can't keep up, so he tells Laurel, "Another fine mess you got me into!"

Laurel pushes him in front of the car. The cops hit Hardy and throws his body in the air. As Laurel's getting away, he gives his buddy a wave. "See you around, fatso!"

The Dickless Soldier

Two cops entered the cell and roused me from my sleep then took me to an interview room and cuffed me to a table. Two detectives sat opposite.

One of them looked down at his notes. "Attempted rape."

I told them I was innocent.

"That's not what we have here."

"It's bullshit."

"Well, why don't you enlighten us."

"Can you keep an open mind?"

"We want only the facts."

"First, can I have a drink of water. My throat is dry."

He sent out a uniform for some water. He came back and placed a cup in front of me. I drank, then told them my story...

"I met a girl in a night club. We went to her place and started making out on the sofa when I hear a noise. I look over by the window and see a pair of shoes under the curtains. I yelled for the pervert to come out!

The curtains parted and a little man with glasses stepped out. 'Is everything alright?'

I threw her off and jumped up. 'What the fuck's going on!'

The pervert smiled. 'Is there something wrong with my wife?'

I yelled, 'Your wife!' I looked around for hidden cameras.

'It's alright. You have my consent.'

I couldn't believe it! He was giving me permission to fuck his wife!

He tilted his head and gave me a concerned look. 'Is there something wrong with the pussy?'

I wanted to slap him sideways! 'That's your wife!'

'Is it money?'

I turned to the girl. 'Are you hearing this!'

'It's alright,' she told me. 'He only wants to make me happy.'

'By getting some stranger fuck you?'

'He used to be a soldier but lost his dick in the war.'

And as if to prove it, he pulled down his pants.

This shit was unreal! I told him to pull them back up before I castrate him again!

She pleaded, 'It's my birthday, and he can't make love to me.'

'Then see a marriage counsellor!'

He looked pale and collapsed on the floor.

I shook my head. 'Really?'

She ran to him and fell on her knees. 'Can't you see that he's sick!' She cradled his head in her arms.

I told them they should have won an Oscar.

She threw a shoe and yelled for me to get out! I told her with pleasure and slammed the door!"

The detectives were laughing.

"Then I went to an all-night café and got a coffee. The woman on the next stool started smiling at me. So, I told her to fuck herself. She screamed rape, someone punched me, and I woke up here."

The detectives were killing themselves laughing.

"I shouldn't be here!"

"It's a ridiculous story."

"So, what happens now?"

"We're letting you off with a warning but keep out of trouble."

"Don't worry," I told them, "I'm joining a monastery."

They started laughing again.

When I left the station, I wasn't joking. I was thinking of becoming a monk.

— *End* —

The Deviously Rich

"I say, it's ghastly what happened to old Beastly."

"That wretched girl broke his heart. So, he took a header off a bridge."

"Goes to say, money can't buy you love."

"But it sure will keep you contented in old age."

"Try telling that to old Beastly."

They both started laughing.

"I say we invite the old girl over for a munch and pat her on the back. It was a stroke of genius getting rid of Beastly like that."

"And who knows, she may let us have our wicked way."

"Steady on, old boy, that's my cousin you're talking about!"

"Alright, you can go first."

"I ought to swipe you with my glove!"

"Jesting, Charles, I'm an officer and a gentleman."

"Nonsense, Piggy, you're a cad and a rogue."

"Takes one to know one."

"I wonder if my cousin has a friend?"

They both started laughing again.

Our Friendly GP

You may think I'm crazy, but I had psychiatric problems growing up. The doctor prescribed chlorpromazine and doxepin. I was on them for years and they did me more harm than good. I was anxious, scared, and confused all the time, and they gave me muscle seizures. I was afraid to go out, but when I was forced to, I was paranoid and thought people were trying to kill me. I kept going back to the doctor, but he treated me like a fool. Once, he gave me sleeping pills and told me to sleep it off. I wanted to bounce his head off the wall! The panic attacks got so bad I was having spasms on the street. Once I was crossing the road and my muscles seized up. Couldn't move. Cars were swerving to avoid me. I thought the doctor was trying to kill me and threw away the pills.

Back at the surgery, the phone rings. The receptionist answers it and tells the doctor he has a call.

"Who is it?"

"Some guy called Robin."

"Has he a last name?"

"Hood. Is this a joke?"

"Put him on."

A voice came on the line. "Is it safe?"

"Is what safe?"

"Is it safe to talk?"

"Hang up and I'll call you back."

The doctor takes out his burner phone and calls him. "It's me."

"Is it safe?"

"I'm getting tired of your damn voice! What is it?"

"The guy you told me to follow nearly got hit by a car."

"Is he dead?"

"What part of 'nearly' don't you understand?"

"Alright, get on with it!"

"And there's more."

"Well, don't keep me in suspense."

"He threw away the pills."

"Are you sure?"

"I'm holding them in my hands."

"Well throw them down the drain, and move onto Plan B."

"What's Plan B?"

"Shoot the bastard."

"It'll cost extra."

"How much?"

"Fifteen G's."

The doctor calls him a thief.

"Well look in the Yellow Pages."

"Alright, have you got a gun?"

"I'm a killer, what do you think?"

"Well get it done!"

I know what you're thinking, *all doctors are saints*. Well tell that to Harold Shipman.

--- *End* ---

Girl walks into her house and meets her mother in the sitting room.

"Mum, I've just met a bloke. I'm bringing him home for tea."

Mother asks, "What does he look like?"

"A beast, but he has money."

So, the mother tells her, "Well let me take out my best dress."

Some people think I'm rude because I joke about crazy shit, but I have an outrageous sense of humour. So, bite me. Sometimes we get involved in crazy stuff that drive us over the edge, but later, when we think about it, we see the funny side. But some stuff can offend the wrong people. Like sex. Some have a religious sensibility about sex. Joke about sex and it's a sin against God. And death can be another taboo subject. If you laugh about death. You have a sadistic mind. Well, I'd like to remind everyone that having a sense of humour is what makes us all smile. So, chill out, take a Valium, and remember, it's not the end of the world. And enjoy.

I've met some crazy people, but there's none crazier than the guys in the next story. And they're claiming to be cops! "Holy shit! Hey, barman, pour me another drink!" Hearing voices and psychotic behaviour is a serious thing. Can you imagine what goes on in the mind of a schizophrenic? Don't answer that, people will know who you are. Anyway, here's a story about a guy and his imaginary friend, called…

Yin and Yang

The detective switched on the tape recorder. "Officer Riley, can you tell us what happened on the day of the shooting?"

"The guy was fucking crazy!"

"Remember, you're on record."

"Sorry. The suspect was in a stolen car. So, we asked him to step out of the vehicle, but he brought out a gun and shot my partner. So, I had to take him down."

"The suspect is dead, and we have only your account of the shooting."

"And my partner's lying in a morgue!"

"So, you're saying it was justified?"

Riley trembled as he remembered the experience. "It was him or me!"

The detective told the time and stopped the tape. Then said to Riley, "Do you need a break?"

Riley shook his head.

"Before we go on. Do you need water or anything?"

"No. I'm alright."

So, he switched the recorder back on.

"Officer Riley, can you tell us what happened on the day of..."

So, Riley recounted his story:

A car screeched around a corner, nearly knocking down a pedestrian and came to a halt. A guy jumped out of the car and ran to the man on the ground.

"You, alright?"

The man threw out his hands to ward off an attack. "What do you want?"

"We're cops. I'm Yin, and that's Yang," said the guy, pointing to his invisible friend, "and we're chasing a crook."

The man thought he was crazy and told him to go away.

Yin got back in the car and opened the door for his partner, but the door was left open. So, he leaned over his partner and closed it for him. "What's wrong with you?"

His partner told him to fuck off. So, he slapped his partner.

A man passing saw Yin and shook his head. "Is there an asylum around here?"

Yin reversed the car and went gunning for him, but the man leapt out of the way like his life depended on it and waved a fist. "Crazy fucker!"

Yin laughed as he drove away.

Two cops were parked by the side of the road having a lunch break. Yin stopped beside them and smiled.

They eyed him suspiciously. "Can we help you?"

He told them he was on the job with his partner, and they were chasing a perp.

They looked at the empty seat and asked where his partner was.

He pointed to his imaginary friend. "Something wrong with your eyes?"

They got out of the car and asked for licence and registration.

Yin told them they were undercover. So, they didn't carry ID.

They studied his face to see if he was on drugs, then got his name and station. Then one cop kept him talking while his partner got on the radio and found out that the car was stolen.

He gave his partner a sign and they brought out their guns. "Sir, you mind stepping out of the car?"

"Hey, what is this?"

"Can you please step out of the car!"

But Yin got nervous and drew out a gun, then everything went crazy…

The detective stopped him. "Officer Riley, is that a true and accurate account of events?"

"I've got nothing to hide. Has anyone seen my partner's wife?"

"It's taken care of. Officer Riley let's concentrate on the matter at hand. You put six bullets in the suspect. Wasn't that a little excessive?"

Riley gave him an angry look. "I was fighting for my goddamn life and my partner was dead!"

The detective looked sympathetic. "We're sorry for your loss," and wrote something in his notes.

"So, what happens now?"

"Thank you, Officer Riley, that will be all. You're suspended from duty with pay until further notice, but I don't see a problem. It was a justifiable shooting. You're free to go."

As Riley left the station his colleagues patted his back.

END

Guards take a man to the electric chair. He's laughing and joking. They shake their heads and tell him, "Still cracking jokes?"

So, he told them, "That's why they call me the Joker."

Bats in the Belfry

"Breaking news! Insane criminals have taken over Arkham Asylum. Here's an announcement from the Joker in Arkham Prison."

"Hi, folks, in case you're wondering where the Bat is. He's a little tied up right now, going a little crazy in a padded cell. Maybe I should up his meds? But as they say in Gotham, that's show business!"

"Joker, what are you going to do with Batman?"

You see Batman lying on a gurney in a straitjacket, and the Joker dancing around him with a toy gun.

"Why don't you tune in next week and find out!" Hysterical laughter can be heard.

Black in America

If a white kid goes missing in New York, it's abduction or murder, but if a Black kid goes missing, it's a runaway. Black kid goes missing in the projects. So, the mother goes to the police. They tell her they're busy and give her the number of a private investigator, but she's poor. So, it takes a year to raise the money to get the PI. He finds out the son's been murdered. So, she goes back to the cops and demands an investigation, but they send her back to the PI for a name. It takes another year, but she goes back to them with the name of the killer, and they tell her to wait for a call. Two years pass and they haven't called. So, she goes back to the station, and they tell her the killer's dead. She asks how? They tell her cancer. She's waited a long time for justice, but it isn't the justice she wants. So, she feels cheated, grabs her chest and has a heart attack. They put her in a cell while they wait for the ambulance to arrive, but it doesn't come for several hours. By that time, she's dead. Now the cops have a problem. They need something to put in the report to explain how she died. So, they ask the ambulance guy what took him so long, and he tells them he was on a date. "The pussy must have been good," joked a cop. "Like cherry pie." And everyone's laughing and joking. But they can't put that in the report. So, they put their heads together and chalk it down to a breakdown of communication.

END

The Little Guy

A killer was terrorizing and killing midgets in New York, and one of the wealthiest men in the city was a little guy. So, he put pressure on the mayor to get him. The mayor put out a big reward and the lines in the precinct were going crazy. A man walked into the precinct and claimed he knew the killer. They went to dismiss him, but he gave them something that could help their case. So, they took him into an interview room and made him wait for a detective. Two came along and sat opposite him at a table. The large cop is Joe, and his skinny partner is Roy, and the guy is Steve.

Joe is asking the questions. "So, you know the guy that's killing all those people?"

"I've met him," said the guy.

"And who's he to you?"

"Just a guy I met."

"And why are you giving him up?"

"I hear there's a reward."

The detective picked up the evidence bag. "You brought us something that only the killer could have had. How do we know you're not our guy?"

"Because I'm going to tell you where to find him."

"First, tell us how you know him."

"I work in a bar. A guy comes in and orders a drink. Closing time, he's drunk and needs someone to take him home. So, he turns to me and says, how would you like to earn 50? I tell him, I don't do that kind of thing. He says all he wants is a lift home. So, I think, why not. Easy money. I take him to his hotel. We get there and he offers me another 20 to take him to his room. The guy could hardly walk. So, I take him to his room and drop him on the bed. As I'm leaving, he offers me a drink. I tell him he's had enough, but he offers me another 20 to keep him company. So, I think, why not…"

The cop stopped him. "You do know that robbery's a crime?"

"I did him a service, and I wasn't breaking any laws."

"And you didn't solicit him for sex?"

The guy felt insulted. "Are you fucking with me? Do you want to hear the story or not?"

"Alright, carry on."

"So, we're drinking, and he falls asleep. As I'm leaving, I decide to use the toilet. I'm washing my hands and see a cupboard over the sink. So, I open it to look…"

"What was you looking for?"

"I wasn't going to steal anything. I just wanted to see what he wears. Like aftershave and stuff. And that's when I found the driving license with the picture of the guy."

"It just happened to be in the cupboard, where everyone can see it?"

"Don't ask me how the guy thinks. And that's when it hit me. It was the dead guy on the news."

"And you recognized him?"

"I'm good with faces."

Roy told him, "That's a fantastic story."

"Yeah, unbelievable, right?"

The cops look at him like he's fucking with them. "Fucking right, it's unbelievable! How do we know you're not the killer or his accomplice?"

"Would I be giving him up if I were?"

"Crazier things have happened," Joe told him.

"Listen, fat boy, I'm doing you a favour! Do you want this guy or not?"

Joe gave him an angry look, but Roy butted in. "Give us the guy's name and where we can find him."

"What about the reward?"

"Maybe if you had the murder weapon, we could give you something up front."

"Then you'll say that I did it."

"Just helping you get your reward."

"Yeah, to prison! You fucks are yanking my chain! Fuck you and your retarded friend!"

Joe went to grab him across the table, but Roy held him back and whispered in his ear.

"Hey, what's going on?"

"You're under arrest," Roy told him.

"On what charge?"

They threw him on the floor and cuffed him.

"Wait a minute!" cried the guy. "I'm trying to help you!"

"Save all that bullshit for court," Roy told him. And they read him his rights.

—— *END* ——

The Cockney Rebels

Two buddies are on an East London council estate, drinking and smoking weed. They haven't seen each other for a while and have a lot of catching up to do. One has a long scar on his face. So, his friend asks, "Who gave you the Mars Bar?"

"Had a barney with five geezers. One of them had a razor."

"Oh, yeah, what happened?"

"Knocked them all out."

"You took on five guys?"

"Laid them out on the ground."

The other guy thinks it's bullshit, but he plays along. "What are you, a ninja?"

He tells him he's more like Rocky.

So, his friend squares up for a fight. "Well, show me some moves."

But he shakes his head. "I wouldn't want to hurt you."

"Don't worry. I can handle myself."

"My hands are a lethal weapon."

His friend laughs and shows him his chin. "Don't be shy. I'll even let you get in the first punch."

But he turns away. "I couldn't hurt a friend."

The other guy calls him a wanker.

"What was that?"

"Do one before I embarrass you!"

He turns around and gives him an angry look. "Say that again?"

"I said, fuck off, lying sack of shit!"

Their mother comes into the garden and sees them wrestling on the ground. She yells, "Why can't you brothers get along! It's time for tea!"

— End —

In the East End there's always some Jack the Lad character the villains go to when they have a problem. This cheeky monkey was handy with a blade. He carried it in a long coat. So, they called him…

Mack the Knife

Mack was sitting at a table in an East End caff eating breakfast. He had eggs, bacon, sausages, beans, toast, and a cup of coffee. A dude came into the café and sat opposite him. His name was Weasel.

Mack looked up from his meal and saw Weasel staring at him. "What's up?"

"The Man wants you to send someone a message."

He carried on eating. "Who is it?"

"Some guy called Scooter."

"Never heard of him."

"Same as before."

"What did he do?"

"It doesn't matter."

"It does if you want me to do him."

"He's a grass."

Mack shook his head. "Naughty boy. Half up front."

Weasel dropped an envelope by his plate.

Mack put the envelope in his pocket. "Where can I find him?"

"Aren't you going to count it?"

"I know where to find you if it's short."

Weasel dropped a photo on the table. "Tonight, a club called the Blue Moon. Know it?"

Mack picked up the photo and looked at it. "I'll find it." He put it in his pocket. "How do you want it done?"

"In the club. We have people there. It'll be busy. So be careful."

"So, why can't they do it?"

"They're not as crazy as you," said Weasel, smiling.

"Good to know I have friends."

"Don't let the Man down," said Weasel, leaving the table.

Mack finished his meal, left the café, and drove home. As he got out of the car, a woman approached him.

"Hey, Mack, you got a minute?"

"What is it, Kerri?" said Mack, locking the car.

"Want you to do me a favour."

Mack entered a block of flats and climbed some stairs. "What's it this time?"

She followed. "My fella's been getting rough. He's using again. I need you to sort him out."

He stopped at a flat, opened the door, and stepped inside. "Why don't you just dump him?"

She closed the door. "Then who would pay the bills?"

"Try working like everyone else."

"Well, are you going to help me?"

Mack went to the kitchen and made some coffee. "It depends."

"On what?"

"On what you can do for me."

"Are you holding?"

"You mean puff?"

"Well?"

"In the bedroom."

She took him to the bedroom and gave him a good seeing to. Then, after, they laid in bed smoking, looking up at the ceiling. He passed her the joint. "You're wasted on him."

"Was that an invitation?"

Mack laughed. "I've got enough grief."

She put a hand between his legs. "Well maybe I can change your mind?"

Mack pushed it away and got out of bed and started putting his clothes on.

"Where are you going?"

"Got somewhere to be."

"Well don't forget. You owe me."

"It's sorted. Lock up when you're done and don't steal anything," said Mack, leaving the flat.

It was after ten when Mack drove to the Blue Moon. He parked around the corner and went to a bar, had a pint, then made his way to the club. There was a bouncer at the door. He barred his way and looked him up and down.

"Shouldn't you be in bed, granddad?"

"Too many coffees."

"Well, behave yourself," said the bouncer, stepping aside.

Mack paid and walked into a hall with flashing lights and loud music. Around him were young people, drinking and prancing around, and it reminded him of his youth.

A pretty girl gyrated her hips and flashed him a smile. "Want to buy me a drink?"

"You better wear some clothes first," Mack told her.

"Less to take off," she teased.

Mack told her to move on.

"Are you queer or something?"

"Now run along before you get hurt."

She saw the menace in his eyes and decided it was good advice.

Mack walked around and saw Scooter on the dancefloor with some friends. He sat and watched them. Scooter left with a friend and went to the toilet.

He followed, waited a few minutes, then entered the toilet. He heard them laughing in a stall.

He banged on the door. "Bouncer! Open-up!"

"Fuck off!" cried a voice.

"You've got till three, then I'm coming in to give you a slap!"

The door opened a crack, and Scooter cussed him with powder on his nose, but when he saw the knife, he tried to close it, but Mack kicked it open and threw him against his friend, then went to work with his blade. They were squealing like pigs. "Stay still, you bastards!" Stripe! Stripe! Stripe! It was embarrassing to watch. Then he left the toilet and walked out the club.

The next day, Weasel found him in the café sitting at the same table, eating the same breakfast. He sat opposite. "Don't they serve anything else?"

"Where's my money?"

Weasel took out an envelope and dropped it on the table. "There's a little extra."

Mack put it in his pocket.

"Don't spend it all at once," said Weasel, getting up to leave.

Mack went back to his food. "Tell the Man it was a pleasure doing business."

Weasel shook his head. "You really love your work, don't you?"

"Somebody has to do it."

"Yeah, evil bastards like you."

Mack grinned like he had been told a joke.

"We'll keep in touch," said Weasel, walking away.

Mack nodded and carried on eating.

END

The Quiet Life

I'm all for a peaceful protest, but some go on the demos because they love the aggro and when people get hurt, they wonder why you're angry and want them out of your area. As if you're an idiot for being upset by the trouble.

"Hey, you come around here, fighting and terrorizing everyone! What's your problem?"

"I hate myself and I don't feel loved."

"So, you want to kill us?"

"And I don't like Mondays."

"Look, I don't mean you any offence but get the fuck out of here!"

Didn't King teach us anything. Chill out, take a Valium, and read *The Beano*. And see a doctor about those demons in your head.

Black Jesus is on a soap box with his arms wide open like he's embracing the world. "People, we all share a common bond. We have the same blood flowing through our veins, and we come from the same place. The only thing that makes us different is the colour of our skin, but search in your hearts. Are we not brothers and sisters?"

A white guy calls from the crowd, "You're saying, I've got Black blood in my body?"

"Welcome to the human race, my friend."

"Shit! I'm getting me a blood transfusion!"

But, joking aside, we're all related and should be kinder to each other. Have you ever been to an AA meeting? Here's another guy apologizing for some bullshit. He's a member of Alcoholic Anonymous and been told to make amends to the people he's wronged. So, he knocks on a door.

A guy answers and recognizes him. "What the fuck do you want?"

"I'm sorry, man. I did you wrong. Will you accept my apology?"

"You're sorry? Are you fucking with me?"

"I broke up with my girl and was having a bad time, and you were in the wrong place."

"I was in the wrong place. That's your fucking excuse?"

"Look, man, I'm sorry." The dude brings out his wallet. "Let me make it up to you."

The guy slaps it out of his hand. "What are you, a wise guy? You lied to the cops and got me eight fucking years, and now you're going to make it up by giving me a few dollars?"

"Come on, man. I said I was sorry. What do you want me to do?"

The guy kicks him down the stairs. "Get the fuck out of here before you lose your life!"

I know what you're thinking. *If I did eight years for some sucker, we wouldn't be having a conversation.* But the guy didn't want to go away for another long stretch. But joking aside, have happy thoughts and remember, don't let the bastards bring you down.

"Hey, where did you think up this bullshit?"

"Read the Good Samaritan's guide."

National Security

Chicago in the state of Illinois, a man walked into an apartment and disturbed a thief. The intruder shot him and left the apartment. A few hours later, another man entered the apartment and called a number. He was put through to another line.

"Yeah?" said a voice on the line.
"Sir, the asset is gone."
"What do you mean, gone?"
"Dead, and the disc is missing."
"Where are you?"
"In his apartment."
"Is this a secure line?"
"Yes, sir."
"I'll make a call. Are you sure?"
"I looked."
"Do we know who?"
"No, sir. Expect a call from the Chicago police."
"Why?"
"I may need clearance."
"Why?"
"I think they're outside."
"Give them the number," said the voice, and the line went dead.

Cops were called to a building where shots were fired. When they entered the apartment, they found a man sitting in a chair with a dead body at his feet. They trained their guns on him. "Don't move!"

He smiled. "Are those necessary?"

"Slowly put your hands in the air!"

He raised his hands.

"Are you armed?"

He shook his head. "There's a gun on the floor. It isn't mine."

"Stand up slowly and keep your hands where we can see them!"

They frisked him and found a wallet and phone.

They looked in the wallet and found a card. No license and no credit cards.

"Then who did it?" enquired the lead cop.

"I found him that way."

He looked at the card. "Who are you?"

"Read the card."

"Who are you?"

He gave them a name. "I work for the government and the gun on the floor isn't the murder weapon. It belonged to the victim."

"How do you know?"

"It hasn't been fired. Ring the number on the card and talk to my superior."

"Who is he?"

"I'm a government employee and that's all you need to know."

"Do you work for a spy agency?"

"Ring the number and speak to my superior."

The cop makes a few calls and is told to let him go. They ask if he's CIA.

"What I am isn't relevant. Can I put my hands down?"

They wave his hands down and give him his wallet and phone.

"What are you doing here?"

"Calling on a colleague."

"You knew the victim?"

"We worked together."

"Doing what?"

The stranger stretches his legs. "Government work."

"Doing what for the government?"

"Take it up with your superiors, but in the meantime, it's been a pleasure, gentlemen."

They stop him from leaving. "This is a crime scene, and we still have questions."

He brings out his phone. "Do we need to make another call?"

The cop shakes his head. "That won't be necessary, sir."

"Then I'm free to go?"

They step aside to let him pass. "But we'll need to know where you are."

"You know where to find me," said the stranger, opening the door.

"Just one more thing."

He turned around.

"Don't leave the country."

The stranger smiled. "You may find this hard to believe but we work for the same side, and we do what is necessary to protect our country. And like you, I'm covered by the Official Secrets Act. It prohibits me from divulging any information that may pose a risk to the security of our country."

"We have a security risk?"

"I'm not at liberty to say."

"Protected from who?"

"Take it up with your superiors. Now, if you don't mind…"

As he leaves, the cop calls his captain and is routed to the White House. He speaks, nods, and ends the call.

His colleague sees the worried look on his face and enquires what's wrong.

"We've been told to vacant the premises. The Secret Service are taking over."

"Can they do that?"

"The government can do whatever they like."

As the stranger steps out of the building, the lead cop follows him through the window and sees him get into a car.

The driver asked, "What happened in there?"

The stranger took his gun out of the glovebox. "We lost the asset and the disc."

"How?"

"He's dead and the disc is gone."

The driver started the engine. "So, what happens now?"

"I make a call."

He called a number, and a voice answered. "Yeah?"

"It's me again, sir."

"You told me this wouldn't happen."

"I can only presume that we have a leak."

"Are you sure?"

"Seems likely."

The line went quiet.

"What would you like us to do, sir?"

"I'll be in touch," said the voice, then the line went dead.

As they drove away, the cop stared out the window like he had seen a ghost.

His partner asked what was wrong.

"I've seen that guy before. He gave us a fake name."

"Then let's arrest him!"

"We can't."

"Why not?"

"He has diplomatic protection."

"Who did you call?"

"The White House."

"The White House?"

He nodded.

"Then who is he?"

"Have you seen James Bond and Jason Bourne?"

"He's a spook?"

He nodded. "And he's responsible for the security of our country."

— END —

Can you imagine what would happen if they stopped the welfare system in England? There would be chaos and anarchy. And for many…

The Beginning of the End

10 Downing Street, London. The chief of staff, Samuel Dexter, was escorted along a narrow corridor by a guard. They stopped at a door. The guard waited. He knocked and was told to enter.

At 52, Dexter was a formidable man, respected and feared by his colleagues, and a close friend of the prime minister.

As he walked into the room, the PM came towards him with an outstretched hand. They shook.

The PM offered him a chair. "How are we today, Dexter?"

"Good, sir, considering our situation."

The PM nodded soberly. "Can I get you a drink?"

"Coffee, sir. Milk, no sugar."

The PM went across the room and came back with a tray. Dexter took a cup from the tray, and the PM took the other.

Dexter told him, "You should have a secretary to do that."

"And overhear all our dirty secrets?" said the PM, smiling.

Dexter brought out a file. The PM picked up a similar file and opened it.

"I wish we were meeting under better circumstances," said the PM, looking grim.

"We keep hoping for a miracle and delaying the inevitable," Dexter told him.

"We're damned if we do and damned if we don't."

"And there's another saying that comes to mind," said Dexter. "Oh, what a tangled web we weave, when we practise to deceive."

"But deceive them we must."

"Whoever said that the truth will set you free didn't consider our situation."

"It's a media nightmare."

"The media is the least of our problems," said Dexter. "Our enemies will take advantage of our weakness and bring the country to its knees."

"So, what do you suggest?"

"The army."

"Martial law?"

"If it gets critical."

"It would turn everyone against us."

"This is bigger than our pride, sir. We have people to protect."

"Put the military on stand-by."

Dexter nodded.

"Have we an exit strategy?"

"Working on it, sir."

The PM nodded and gave his friend a look of resignation. "Then it's only a matter of time. The welfare system will have to be abolished, but the question is how?"

END

I bet you're waiting for Bruce Willis to jump out of a helicopter in a military uniform and declare martial law. Well let's hope it never happens.

"Shit! They're storming the building! Has anyone seen Denzel Washington?"

"You mean the action guy in the movies?"

"Yeah, the *Equalizer* bloke."

"He went out the back door."

The Coronavirus

The coronavirus first started in China in 2019, and has escalated around the world, and we are fighting desperately to find a cure. Many have died in England, and more are dying every day. Our government has told us not to worry. They have it under control. But that was over a year ago. Since then, thousands have succumbed to the disease, and we are running out of graves. They're cremating bodies on the street to stop the contamination. No one wants to care for the sick or bury the dead. So, we turn our backs on our friends. God help us all. It's pitiful what we've become.

Today is October 23, 2021. Now that the virus has gone airborne, it's an offence not to wear a mask. Those that disobey are endangering lives and putting others at risk. So, they are regarded as criminals. They're taken to camps where they are tortured and abused. We call them death camps because they never come out alive. It's meant to serve as a deterrent to keep us in line, but it has only made us more vigilant and now we carry guns.

Hospitals are overwhelmed and understaffed. They cry for help and supplies, but their pleads are rejected and their voices go unheard. Shops and businesses have stopped trading, leaving millions unemployed. Families go hungry and many turn to crime. Now people pray to a God they have forsaken because they're lonely and afraid. The future is uncertain and uncertainty breeds fear. This madness is affecting us all.

There are food banks to help the poor, but many suffer in silence because they're too scared to leave their homes. I was hungry and my cupboards were bare. So, I donned a coat and conceal a gun but couldn't find a mask. I looked everywhere but it was lost. So, I put a cloth over my nose and went outside.

It was like a ghost town as I walked along the street. Quiet and deserted. And then I heard a cry. "Halt there!"

When I turned around, two masked men with guns and white overalls were coming towards me.

I froze.

"Why aren't you wearing a mask?"

I told them I had lost mine and was picking some up at the food bank. They asked to see some identification, so I showed them my driving license.

He looked at the license and studied my face. Then he got on the radio, while his partner covered me with a gun.

Then he turned back to me. "You do know it's an offense not to wear a mask?"

I told them I didn't have a choice.

He brought out his cuffs and told me to turn around and put my hands behind my back. When I tried to protest, he jabbed me with the gun. "Don't make me ask you again!"

But I wasn't going to a death camp, so I pulled out my gun and took one of them down, but when I turned to the other, I got a bullet in the gut and tapped in the head. Then he called for assistance.

As I laid dead, smiling, he gave me a funny look. I was liberated and free. All my troubles were behind me, and I could finally rest in peace.

End

The Greater Good

The man placed the object on the table. Blake, the guy opposite, was apprehensive. He had never touched a real gun.

"It's all right," said the man. "Pick it up. It will not bite you."

As Blake handled the gun, cold sweat appeared on his forehead.

The man gave him an encouraging smile. "And try not to look nervous. It will only make you look suspicious."

It was night when Blake left the building and entered the street. The sidewalk was busy with people. He kept his head down and avoided the eyes as he walked to his car and drove to his destination and parked outside a tall Victorian building. He left the car and made his way to the house, inserted a key in the door and opened it. Then he stepped inside. Blake thought about what he was about to do, and a chill ran down his spine. It seemed like a surreal dream as he followed a dark passage to a room and opened the door. Light from the moon filtered through an un-curtained window. In the semi-darkness, he strained to see the creature in a corner. It was sensitive to light.

I can read your thoughts, said a voice in his head. *And I can sense a sadness.*

Then you know how I feel, Blake spoke back with his mind.

But you have no choice, said the telepathic creature. *It isn't right.*

The creature felt sympathy for the human. *Inside me is a virus. If I were to live, your world would suffer an unimaginable fate. Billions of your people would die. So, you see, their fate is in your hands.*

We could learn so much from each other.

I was sent to kill you.

But why are you willing to die for us?

We thought humans were a cruel and savage race. And we saw the coming of your kind and the destruction of our world. But we were wrong. There is goodness in you. I see compassion and kindness.

In our world, there are good people and bad people.

And this God that you think about. Tell me about him.

He represents what is good in our world, and we are guided by his principles.

And where is this God?

All around us.

Is he here?

He's a presence that we cannot see.

Then your God would want you to save your world.

But there must be another way.

It ends with me. Do what must be done and may your God be with you.

Blake felt a deep sense of sadness and loss, but he knew that the creature was right. So, he raised the gun and pointed it at the creature. *And may God be with you.* He wiped his eyes and pulled the trigger.

End

Death

The psychiatrist sat in his chair by the window and looked up at the sky. It was a grey and dismal day, much like his life. Gone was the ambition to heal the sick and needy minds. Now it all seemed so trivial. His clients were their own worst enemies who complicated their lives with unnecessary problems. It took him 16 years to discover the truth and now he was disillusioned and tired.

Nine o'clock. The intercom announced his first appointment. The man was in his 30s, married with two children, and on the verge of divorce. He argued with his wife constantly and feared she was having an affair. And blamed himself. The psychiatrist listened to his unfounded suspicions, gave advice, and made another appointment.

The intercom announced his ten o'clock appointment. An attractive woman in her 40s who had relationship problems. She suffered with anxiety, worried constantly, and was socially awkward. He sympathized with her, wrote a prescription, and made another appointment.

Eleven o'clock. A man in his early 20s came into the room. He sat opposite and complained about his problems. He was antisocial and thought the world was against him. The psychiatrist listened patiently and gave some advice.

Then he waited for his next appointment.

He heard a knock, and a young woman came in. She was pretty and in her 20s. He offered her a chair and looked down at his notes.

"Fear of dying," he told her.

"Fear of Death," she corrected him.

"I fail to see the difference?"

"The Death I refer to has a face."

He decided to humour her. "And what does Death look like?"

"It can take on many forms and look like you or me."

"I see," said the doctor, trying not to smile. "And has Death appeared to you?"

"On many occasions."

"And what does it want?"

"For me to pass on a message."

"To whom?"

"You."

"A message for me?"

"That you are going to die."

The psychiatrist seemed amused but reminded himself that the patient was ill. So, he considered the patient with pity and wrote 'personality disorder' in his notes and when he looked up, she was holding a gun.

Death gave the doctor a twisted smile.

End

You're thinking, *that's creepy!* Well let me tell you what happened when I saw my psychiatrist.

"Doctor, there's a guy with a bat clubbing people."
"It's all in your head."
"Well, imagine this." Whack! Whack! Whack!

Winter in July

It was a nice evening. My baby and I had just watched a movie and were going home from the cinema when a man stepped out of an alley with a gun.

He smiled and pointed it at us. "Nice night for a stroll."

"We're not looking for trouble," I told him.

"Play nice and you won't get hurt."

I gave him my wallet and watch.

Then he turned to my baby. "You too, doll. Don't be shy"

She gave him her bag and told him to choke on it.

He laughed. "The rings too."

She told him that one of them was a present from her dead father.

He waved the gun impatiently. "Maybe you'd like to join him."

She took them off her fingers. "How can you sleep at night!"

He told her, "I sleep just fine," then shot me in the stomach and made off with his haul.

As I hit the ground, clutching my stomach, blood was seeping through my fingers. My baby fell beside me and rocked me in her arms.

"Don't close your eyes!" she screamed. "Stay with me! Stay with me!"

But I was numb and drifting in and out of consciousness. "Stay with me!"

I could see angels all around me, dancing, flying in the sky. I beckoned for the angel to sing for me and heard her sweet soothing voice…

When I opened my eyes, I was floating through a dark empty void. A vast expanse of nothingness. It was warm like a mother's womb, and I felt safe, like I had nothing to fear. And in the darkness was a light. A small light that started to grow and as I glided towards it. It shimmered and glowed. And there was a tunnel in the light. A long oblong shape. And at the entrance of the tunnel was a man. As I got nearer, I could see that it was an old man in a white robe with a warm, friendly face. He smiled and opened his arms, and as I drifted into his arms, embraced me like we were old friends. Then led me into the light, and as we walked through the tunnel, side by side, it felt like I was going home.

— *End* —

You're probably looking out the window, waiting for the Grim Reaper to come and get you. Well enough of the gloom and doom. Here's something that will make you smile.

Man's Best Friend

Guy hears his neighbour calling as he's getting into his car with his dog. So, he turns around.

The neighbour waves. "Hi, John, where are you going?"

"Taking the dog for a walk."

"In the car? There's a park down the road."

"Got to go somewhere first."

So, he drives off and takes the dog to a field. The dog's jumping around like he wants to play. So, he throws a stick. When the dog comes back with the stick, the owner is gone. John sees a friend, then drives home. As he's getting out of the car, his neighbour is smoking by his door.

"Alright, John, where's the dog?"

John looks sad like he's lost a best friend. "He ran away."

"Shouldn't you be looking for him?"

"It's too dark. I'll try again in the morning."

His neighbour tells him, "That's funny, because he's in my house."

John acts relieved. When the neighbour opens his door, the dog runs out and starts biting him.

END

I like to use words that compliment my characters and keep the pace and momentum moving. It's the words you use and the way you say it. Some people think you need a fancy plot to tell a story, but you can make a good story out of anything. It's how you put it across. Like with just two guys in a room. Just keep it simple. You don't have to overdo it with a baffling plot and difficult words. People just want to follow an easy story. Something they could relate to in their own language, not get bored and interrupted by complicated details. You're reading for pleasure. It isn't rocket-science. So, just relax and enjoy yourself.

Let it Flow

Boy in classroom writes a story and shows it to the teacher, but the teacher tells him it needs more work. So, he works on it and brings it back to the teacher, but it needs more details. So, he adds more details and takes it back, but it needs more structure. The kid's been up and down and all he's getting is a hard time. So, he's frustrated and tired. He tells the teacher, "It has a plot, tells the story, and the characters are good. What more do you want?"

"Is it night or day? Are they here or abroad? And what clothes are they wearing?"

So, the kid told him, "It's a short story about two guys in a room, drinking and telling jokes."

— END —

Oh, how sweet it feels to have wings to fly. To sail around Heaven on a clear blue sky.

Monsters and Demons

In 15th century Romania, a man had created a formula that made him invisible and was killing people he deemed enemies of the state. Lawyers, politicians, doctors, and now he was murdering priests. He claimed the churches had too much power and were using their influence to corrupt the country. His latest victims were from the Vatican. So, the Vatican sent from for Van Helsing, the most feared monster slayer in Europe, to have an audience with the pope.

Helsing stood before the pope and bowed. "Monsignor."

The pope sat behind his desk and waved for him to sit, but Helsing remained standing.

"Why have you summoned me?"

"Are you familiar with the Invisible Man?"

"I've heard rumours."

"And what have you heard?"

"He kills priests."

"We have lost four from the Vatican."

The pope told Helsing about the Invisible Man's threat to the church and the damage it was doing to their reputation.

"And what would you like me to do?"

"Take care of our problem."

"I kill monsters and demons."

"Then you are the man for the job."

"How do you kill an enemy you cannot see?"

The pope considered it and told Helsing, "You set a trap."

Van Helsing disguised himself as a blind old man with dark glasses and a cane and tapped his way into a tavern. He sat at the bar and ordered a drink. Then he turned to man on the next stool and engaged him in a conversation. He was an old man like himself, so he welcomed a chat. They small talked for a while, then the blindman talked about the pope and how he had sired a child with a prostitute.

"How can that be?" said the man, nearly choking on his drink.

"The pope has orgies in the Vatican."

The man looked at him like he was mad. "That's blasphemy! How can you say that about the pope!"

"I was there when the girl was born."

The man had to force himself not to laugh. "And I suppose you were a fly on the wall?"

"A fly with proof."

"What proof?"

"Documents from the birth."

The man decided to humour him. "And how did you get them?"

"I stole them from the pope."

The man stopped drinking and looked hard at his face. "Who are you?"

"I was a priest at the Vatican, excommunicated for my belief."

"But you are blind?"

"They made me blind for speaking my mind."

"And where are the papers?"

"In a safe place."

"But a scandal like that could ruin the church!"

By the time the blindman left the tavern, everyone was talking about the pope and his illegitimate child.

As he tapped his way along the street, he heard a voice. "Why do you lie?"

He stopped and tapped the ground around him with the cane. "Who's there?"

The Invisible Man repeated the question. "Why do you lie about the pope?"

The blindman sniffed the air as if he could smell the stranger. "And how do you know that I lie?"

"Women are not allowed in the Vatican. It is forbidden."

The blindman laughed. "Then we are both fools."

A woman went by and saw the blindman talking to himself and wondered if he was mad.

"These documents," said the Invisible Man. "Where are they?"

"Are you a spy for the church?"

"No, old man, but I can be a very useful friend."

The blindman huffed. "I have plenty of friends."

The Invisible Man laughed. "I see them beating down your door. How much do you want?"

"And what makes you think you could bribe me?"

"Everyone has a price."

The blindman held out a hand.

The Invisible Man put a coin in it.

The blindman bit the coin and held out for another.

"You drive a hard bargain," said the Invisible Man, putting another coin in his hand. "And there's plenty more where that came from."

"Then follow me," said the blindman, tapping his way down the street.

They turned onto a quiet road and stopped at a house. The blindman pushed open the door.

The Invisible Man wondered if he was lost. "Wait! Is this your home?"

"I can show you the deeds."

"But you are blind?"

"And my senses are good."

"And where are your keys? Aren't you worried that someone would rob you?"

"I have nothing to steal," said the blindman, taking him into the house.

"Except the papers."

"They are in a safe place. And my nose is sharp. I can smell a crook a mile away."

"And what do I smell like?"

The blindman told him money.

The Invisible Man laughed and followed him into the kitchen. "Old man, you joke with me, but I like you. You have a sense of humour."

The blindman made him sit at a table and brought over a jug and two glasses. "Join me for some beer."

"Some other time. Where are the papers?"

"We must seal the deal with a drink," said the blindman. "You insult me if you don't."

The Invisible Man laughed, "Alright, just one," and took a glass.

The blindman smiled and filled both glasses, and as they drank, they talked about his role in the Vatican, and how he became a confidant to the Pope. Then he went to find the papers. When he came back, the Invisible Man was pale and sweating.

"Are you alright?" asked the blindman.

But he was stiff like a scarecrow. Unable to move. He looked at the glass. "What did you give me?"

Van Helsing took off the disguise and threw paint on the Invisible Man.

"You've been poisoned and now we'll wait for you to die."

The Invisible Man was perplexed. "But you had the same drink?"

Helsing showed him a vial. "And I also have the antidote."

Van Helsing went back to the Vatican and dropped the Invisible Man's head on the pope's desk.

The pope smiled. "I see you've been busy."

"I believe you have something for me."

The pope told him, "There's a rumour about my illegitimate child."

"I know nothing about it."

The pope smiled and shook his head. "I should hang you for slander."

"Whoever you send better make their peace with the Lord."

The pope laughed and dropped a pouch on the desk. "You were a promising student. Come back to the church. Your talents are needed here."

"I work better alone," said Helsing, picking up the pouch.

"Well, keep in touch. We may need you for another job."

"You know where to find me," said Helsing, bowing and leaving the room.

End

Many have written about Van Helsing, the legendary monster slayer. This is just another take with a touch of comedy. I hope you've enjoyed it as much as I have. And no offense to the Vatican or the pope, who I'm guessing is sitting behind a desk rolling a joint…

Pope: "That dude's got balls. Let's sign him up. What's his name?"

"You mean, the writer?"

Pope: "He's got stones. I'm going to make him a Made Guy."

"Shouldn't we okay it with Al Capone?"

Pope: "He can kiss my ass. I answer to the big guy in the sky."

The boys are drinking and talking about the Pope:

"I hear the Pope's letting some shine into our gang."

"Can you imagine taking orders from a nigger?"

"Holy, mother of God!"

"Hey, Jackie, I hear you like black pussy and soul food. Can you fix me up?"

"Fuck you!"

It gets a few laughs.

"Soon he'll have us smoking crack with the brothers from Harlem."

"That shit ain't right!"

"I say we put a hit on the guy."

"Which one, the pope or the nigger?"

The priests are laughing again.

Poor Little Caesar

My friend, if you're feeling low and on the brink of despair, it may seem as if there is very little meaning to your life. You may feel lost, demoralized, forlorn, wretched and without hope, and welcome death and long for it in anticipation.

As you stare off into oblivion, the wrath of vengeance you have for your foes may feel like a burning venom upon your tongue. When you peer out of the window, the weather will mirror your thoughts, and it may seem as if the Gods are jeering and laughing at their humour creation. So, you throw your fists in the air and declare war on them!

"Oh, cruel and malignant Gods, why must you torture me so! Lead my feet to their poor weary doom and have mercy on my soul!"

But they torment you with their silence, and tease you with their taunt, until you hear a voice. "Hush, hush, little warrior, and don't despair. You have power and riches, what more could you want?"

"But I am lonely, and I have no one to share it with."

"If you were to go now, who would entertain the Gods? Is it not better to reign on Earth than to perish in Hell? For you are a cruel and callous villain in a harsh and ruthless world, and you must rule with a gun. There is work to be done!"

Caesar hung his head and cried.

In a Godless World

The Trianon robots marched as an infestation of hungry maggots ate their master's carrion remains. In thousand they marched, while the soil and dirt shed vampire heads like poison cabbages with green, slimy, disfigured skulls. Masses of mindless zombies forged their way towards the Crimson Walls, looking for food behind the unmarked tombs as a grey mist travelled slowly over the ugly distorted creatures that moved carelessly through the ruins of the planet Zebulon.

Hideous foul beasts devoured each other in a frenzied rage, dragging their bodies through a sea of blood. While the weak hid and gradually withered away in a shrouded cave, they would cry for the Diamond Dog.

When you write science fiction about other worlds you can make up your own rules. The laws of physics don't apply. It is your creation. Your world. There could be castles in the sky. And death can appear in any form.

A Wager with Death

Since the beginning of time there has been conflict between two sides. Good and evil. Angels and demons. For thousands of years, it was agreed that neither side would interfere in the affairs of humans and an uneasy truce was forge. Then, one day, a demon warlord fell in love with an angel princess and a baby was born. Half demon, half angel. And it was foretold that the child would one day possess the powers of a god, and whoever possessed the baby would decide on their fate. So, fearing the loss of their dominion, the demons sent hunters to kill them, but they were protected on Earth by angels. So, a battle was fought with humans caught in the middle, and everyone died. Except for one. A human by the name of Zorach.

Zorach, you were once a protector of women and children, and the proud leader of men, but now if you look around, the sole survivor of a cruel and savage war. But what of you, my brave warrior, why should you endure the pain and suffering of your people. Why should you, and you alone weep for the dead. What will thou do? Where will thou go? Now the roads are deserted, and the forest no longer heeds your call. The air was polluted with death, the sea was red with blood, and Zorach was all alone.

Zorach woke up in a forest. Perplexed, he wondered how he had got there. Beside him was a strange piece of metal the colour of gold. He picked it up and looked at it.

"Lovely, isn't it," said a voice.

Zorach looked around but could see no one. "Who's there?"

"It is I, Death, and I come as a friend."

Zorach stood and raised the sword. "Then, Death, reveal yourself."

From behind a tree, a small ugly creature appeared. Its face resembled that of a fiendish serpent.

It smiled at Zorach.

"What manner of beast are you?" cried Zorach.

As if in answer, the creature produced a flower in its clawlike hand and offered it to Zorach. "This is the resurrection of death. An everlasting peaceful sleep. It knows not fear, worry, nor pain. So, join me, my friend, and be content."

But Zorach was baffled by these riddled words. So, he laughed at the creature. "Fool! You know not what you say!"

"Then humour me and play a game."

"What trickery is this?"

"The sword or your soul."

"Bah!" cried Zorach. "You take me for a fool!"

"Then keep the sword and prove me wrong."

Zorach was tired of the creature. "Begone before I take your head!"

"Do you really want to test me, Zorach?"

"I said begone!"

"You have one day to decide."

Zorach swung the sword and made for the creature's head but, to his amazement, the creature had disappeared.

Zorach thought his eyes were playing tricks with him. He slashed the air, searching for the creature. "Monster, where art thou? Come back and face the wrath of Zorach!"

But, alas, the forest was quiet, the trees were calm, and nothing stirred in the shadows. The creature was gone.

END

When I moved out of London, someone asked me what it was like living on the Old Kent Road. I told them, "I'm still having flashbacks about the Vietnam War. I wouldn't recommend it." It's bandit territory. Go there at your own peril and bring a balaclava and a gun. People who play Monopoly wonder why it's the cheapest place on the board. Try living there. And here's something for all you holy people. When God created the world in six days, he forgot the Old Kent Road. I'm kidding. Pay me no mind. The Millwall fans are nice people. Just wear a crash helmet when you pass them.

"Hey, fucker, I've been trying to sell my house for six months and because of your article, no one will buy it!"

"Yeah, about that. Take it easy, sucker."

Here's a tale about two lost souls who go on a crime spree like Bonnie and Clyde. It's called…

See You on the Other Side

Someone once asked, "Why didn't you live a better life?"

I shrugged, and told them, "You make it up as you go along." But the question that they should have asked was how it all began.

I was born on the 4th of July 1950 in Brooklyn, New York. It was Independence Day, a day of celebration and a time to spread joy. While Mother lay on the hospital bed, cradling me in her arms, Father was pacing about like a nervous wreck, wearing out his shoes.

Mother told him, "You're scaring the baby."

But Father couldn't stand still. "What shall we call him?"

"I quite like Henry."

"The kids will tease him at school."

"Then you name him."

"I don't know."

"We've got to put something on the birth certificate."

"Let me think!"

"Honey, sit down."

But Father decided he needed a drink. "Maybe I'll go for a walk. Is Champagne good for you?"

"Can we afford it?"

"Damn it, woman, we've just had a baby!"

So, Father went out to get some booze. When he stepped in the shop, two crooks were robbing it with guns. One knocked Father to the floor, while his partner yelled at the storekeeper to open the till. "Hurry up! Hurry up!"

But the poor guy was so nervous, he kept pressing the wrong key, and when he got the till open, kept dropping the money. So, the crook thought, *what the hell!* and started blasting. Then he shot Father for being a witness, and by the time the cops showed up, Father was dead, and the crooks were long gone.

When Mother got the news, she broke down and cried, locked herself in a toilet and committed suicide. They must have thought it was a family curse. I was fostered around, deemed an awkward and difficult child, and sent to an orphanage. It was a heartless place where you had to be cruel to survive. The weak were bullied and abused, and the ones that made it through were damaged goods.

On my 18th birthday, they cut me loose without a friend in the world. Gave me $10, a bus ticket, and directions to a halfway house. On the street there were happy bums, merry drunks, and smiling faces, and everyone was celebrating because it was the 4th of July.

In 1969, three fellow Americans landed on the moon, cult leader, Charles Manson, murdered five people, at 47, American actress Judy Garland died of a drug overdose, and a Republican named Richard M. Nixon became the 37th president of the United States. He made empty promises and offered us seedless dreams, but in the radical hippy days of flower power and free love, everyone was too stoned to give a damn. And then there was the Vietnam War.

I was sitting at a bar, minding my own business, when a dame sat on the next stool, and asked me for a light.

I lit her and carried on drinking.

"You mine?"

I looked around and enquired, "Mine what?"

"Mind a little company?"

She was a damsel in distress, so I shrugged. "Be my guest."

She offered me a cigarette, but I declined. "Maybe later."

"I like this bar," she told me.

I shrugged. "It's alright."

"Do you come here much?"

"Are you a regular?"

She nodded.

"Well, you'd know."

She smiled and shook her head. "Wise guy."

It was quiet for a moment, then she started again. "So, what's a nice guy like you doing here?"

"This and that," I told her.

"You're a mysterious guy."

"Got a problem with that?"

"It's your life." She blew smoke pass my face. "Got any plans for later?"

I ordered another drink and told her she was moving too fast.

"Don't you like girls?"

"I like them a little shy."

"Well, pardon me. So, what do you do when you're not drinking alone?"

I told her I was a thief to see how she'd take it.

"Are you a good one?"

I shrugged. "It has its moments."

She laughed and shook her head. "Well stick around. Maybe you'll get lucky."

I nodded and turned it around. "So, what do you do?"

"This and that," she said, smiling.

I nodded like I understood.

"Shall we start again." She held out a hand and told me her name.

I shook it and told her mine.

So, we got talking and time rolled by. Closing time, the bartender rang the bell for last orders.

"Your place or mine?" she told me.

"My place is a mess."

"My place it is."

As we stood to leave, she told me, "I like you, Joe. Maybe you'll grow on me."

I told her it was nice to be liked, and she took me home.

The following morning, I woke up on a strange bed next to a beautiful dame. I had to slap my face to make sure I wasn't dreaming.

She opened her eyes and smiled. "Hi."

"Hi." I smiled back.

"Sleep well?"

"Like a baby, and you?"

She snuggled up to me and kissed my nose. "Like a baby. Did the earth move?"

"Like an earthquake."

She smiled. "So, where do we go from here?"

"Where would you like it to go?"

"Let's take it slow and easy."

I nodded. "That's fine with me."

I got out of bed and started putting on my clothes.

"Where are you going?"
"Thought you might need some space."
"Why, is there another woman?"
"I only have eyes for you."
"Well, why don't you stick around?"
"You sure?"
"Would I be asking?"
"Okay, baby, we'll play it your way."
She rolled on top of me, and we made love.

And that was how it all began. By day, I'd be with my baby, and at night, looking for a mark to rob. The drunks would roll out of a bar, feeling clumsy, and I'd be behind them with a gun.

I'd tap on their shoulder and say, "Nice night for a stroll."

He'd look at the gun, and there'd be fear in his eyes. So, I would offer some advice. "Play it cool and you won't get hurt."

Once, a mark tried to get wise. So, I had to shoot him in the leg, but usually it was like taking candy from a baby. And there were plenty of laughs.

I caught one drunk staggering down the road and waved my gun in his face.

"I'm not looking for trouble!" he cried.

"Listen up, old man, all I want is your dough and I'll be on my way."

"I ain't got no money!"

"Well let me shoot you and find out."

"Alright! Alright!"

He gave me his wallet, and I pointed at rings on his fingers. "Those too, pop."

"Want to bleed me dry?"

"Or I could prise them off your dead fingers."

"Alright! Alright!"

He removed the rings and told me, "I hope you choke on them!"

I gave him a wave as I was leaving. "Take it easy, sucker."

"Fuck you too!" he cried after me.

And there was another guy that threw a punch at me. I knocked him on his ass and waved the gun in his face. "Listen, fool, this is a real gun with real bullets. Don't end up in the morgue."

He threw out his hands like it was a gangland execution. "Don't kill me! Don't kill me! I'll give you anything you want!"

I took his money and left him on the ground. "Next time, I'll charge you extra for the bullet."

One drunk nearly had me feeling sorry for him. He feared the wife more than me.

"The wife will kill me if I'm late!"

I told him, "She won't have to if you're dead."

"Give me a break!"

"Stop fucking around and hand over the dough!"

He rubbed his chin like he was thinking about it. "Alright, let's make a deal."

"You want to negotiate?"

"I'll give you half."

I had to stare hard at him to make sure he wasn't joking. "Are you fucking with me? I ought to cap your ass!"

"Alright! Alright!" he yelled, giving me his money.

Then I made him walk home naked for being a wise guy.

"Get out of here, you bum and tell the wife you got rolled by a hooker!"

Then there was the guy that tried to run. I fired a bullet over his head and stopped him in his tracks.

He turned around and held up his hands. "What do you want?"

"What's wrong with you? Have you got rocks in your head?"

"Look, mister, I'm just trying to get home! I have a sick wife and children!"

I told him, "And don't forget the mortgage and the dog. Empty your pockets!"

"Let me go and I won't say nothing."

I went to clout him with the gun, but he covered his head.

"I surrender!" he cried, bringing out his wallet.

"Relax. This ain't Pearl Harbor."

"Can you leave me a few dollars?"

I snatched it out of his hand. "What am I, a bank?"

"You have a rotten heart."

I laughed and asked if he had far to go.

"Yeah," he told me, "A divorce court!"

That sucker had me rolling so much I was blind walking down the road.

And later I'd be with my baby, and she'd be purring in my arms.

She seemed a little off. So, I asked why.

She told me, "There has to be more to life."

I rubbed her shoulder. "We've got each other. Isn't that enough?"

"But we don't do nothing. Go nowhere."

"I'm happy with the way things are."

"And that's your problem. You don't think big."

"What brought this on, baby?"

"It feels like I'm wasting away."

I kissed her neck. "Don't talk like that, baby."

"There has to be more."

"I'll try harder and we'll have more."

"Or we could rob a bank."

I told her it was crazy talk.

"We'd be like Bonnie and Clyde."

"And look what happened to them."

"But didn't they have fun along the way."

"I can think of better ways to die."

"Or maybe you're scared."

I told my baby I wasn't scared of anything.

"Then prove it. But I'll understand if you're yellow."

I pulled back my hand to slap her. "Call me a coward one more time!"

But she held my gaze and challenged me with her eyes. "Then show me you're not a pussy."

I didn't like being called a pussy. So, I told her it was on.

It was a bright day. We were in a field practising with our guns. My baby put a tin can on a wall and asked if I could hit it.

"Piece of cake," I told her. I aimed at the target and fired, but the bullet went wide.

Tried again and missed by a mile. I made an excuse that the gun didn't feel right.

My baby told me to watch and learn.

She pulled the trigger and knocked the can off the wall. Fired again and made it jump in the air.

I was impressed. "Where'd you learn to shoot like that?"

"My daddy used to take me hunting. He wanted a boy, and they got me."

"Well, you're better than any guy I know."

When she didn't answer, I put my hands on her shoulders and made her face me. "Did he do something to you?"

She turned away and told me to forget it.

But I wanted to know. "Baby, whoever hurts you, hurts me."

"You mean that?"

"Don't you know me by now?"

So, she told me a story about an abusive father who raped and victimized his daughter. When she finished, I didn't know what to say. So, I just looked at her.

"I disgust you now, don't I?"

I pulled her into my chest and looked into her eyes. "You could never do that, baby. I'm just so mad, I want to kill him!"

"Well get in line."

"And where was your mother?"

"She died trying to protect me."

I wanted to know more but she wouldn't talk about it. There were tears in her eyes.

I tried to put my arms around her, but she pushed me away.

"I don't need your pity!"

"Baby, I just want to be there for you."

"She'd still be alive if I didn't say anything!"

"You were only a child."

"A child that should have known better!"

"It could have been you."

She pointed the gun and aimed at an imaginary target. "Well, that bastard will get what's coming."

I told her vengeance won't bring her back.

"But it sure would make me feel good," she told me, walking away.

And that was how we became partners in crime. The first bank we hit, I was a bundle of nerves, but I had a dame to impress. So, I puffed out my chest and acted tough. The second got a little easier, and by the third, it was a walk in the park. The guns in our hands gave us the power to do whatever we wanted.

"Now listen up! It's not your money we're after! Your money is insured! Just do like we ask, and no one will get hurt! Think about your families and friends and this will soon be over!"

I'd wave the gun around and give them a menacing look. The ants would be on the floor, looking beaten and sore. And my baby would be over by the tellers having the time of her life. "Hi, can I make a withdrawal? Put everything in the bag! Hurry up, hurry up!"

"Even the coins?" asked a trembling lady.

"Want to slow me down for the cops? Only the paper! Hurry up, hurry up!"

Then we'd hightail it out of there with the loot and the wheels burning.

"It's a pleasure doing business! Have a nice day, and don't forget to vote!" Man, what a rush!

In the car, she'd give me a funny look, "Did we forget something?"

"Did you?"

"Haven't they got a vault?"

My baby was a barrel of laughs.

In two years, we have robbed 11 banks and are wanted in five states, but now, in the dead of night as I peer out the window, I knew it was only a matter of time.

"You are surrounded! Throw down your weapons and come out with your hands up, and you will not be harmed! I repeat, surrender, and you will not be harmed!"

I asked my baby if she had any regrets.

She told me if she had to do it all again, she wouldn't change a thing.

It made me smile. "We were good together, weren't we."

"The best. But all good things must come to an end."

I told her, "I wouldn't have it any other way. Maybe I'll see you in the next life."

She told me we were going to a better place. Utopia, where we'd be together forever.

I let my baby dream and smiled. "Guess I'll see you on the other side."

"It isn't goodbye."

I looked into those mesmerizing green eyes and gave her an encouraging smile. "It isn't goodbye."

"Are you ready?"

I raised my gun and told her, "As ready as I'll ever be."

"Well, let's go out in style."

We went on both sides of the two windows and looked across at each other one last time before we smashed the glass and poke our guns through the jagged holes and started firing. And all hell broke loose!

End

Don't you enjoy a story with a happy ending. I almost went hopping to a bank with a gun but, knowing my luck, the cops would be waiting outside.

"Throw out your gun and come out with your hands above your head! You have two minutes!"

Shit! How did the cops get here so fast? "Who gave me up?"

"It was your priest!"

And I promised that sucker half the money! "Tell that fucker I'll see him in Hell!"

I know, you're probably wondering if I've got a beef with the banks. Well, I've got nothing against them, long as they give me their money. But joking aside, where would we be without banks? And try robbing one today. They'd laugh you out the door. "Next time, sucker, bring a computer!" But seriously, I hope it was fun and stay tuned for the next story.

Open Season

Imagine that there are other worlds like ours beyond this world. Worlds within worlds, within a multiverse. Some may consider it a science fiction fantasy, but to an analytical mind it's a scientific possibility. Now, imagine New York in a parallel world…

A man goes to work from a hot date and sees everyone worried and agitated. So, he asks, "What's going on?"

"Haven't you heard? Trump won the election!"

He thinks they're punking him. So, he tells them to fuck off. But one guy's jumping around like his house is on fire. "They made him president for another term!"

He shakes his head and tells them, "It's too early in the morning and I haven't had my coffee. Fuck off with your bullshit."

"If you don't believe me, look out the window!"

He looks out the window and sees the police shooting people and waving banners. "Welcome to Purge City!"

Trump is sitting on a car, looking around. "Hey, where did that fucker go?"

"What fucker?"

"The Mexican with the straw hat?"

"Over here, Mr President! He's getting away!"

"Quick, lend me a gun!"

I know what you're thinking. Not in a million years! Crazy talk like that will get you locked up in a funny farm. And the Yankees are too intelligent to be hoodwinked by a crazy zealot like Trump, but bullshit has been known to happen. Especially in America.

— End —

You're probably thinking, *where's the yacht, Lamborghini, and the dancing girls?* Sorry to disappoint you. Ask me what I had for dinner last night and I'll tell you a microwave meal, but that's just me. I'm just a humble writer. So, if you see me looking like a down and out in my rags, stop by and say hello. You're probably waiting for me to tell you that I'm the greatest guy in the world. Well, sorry to disappoint you again. I'm just an average Joe trying to get by with a smile and a helping hand. "Dirty bastard! Get your hands off my tits!"

"Sorry, ma'am."

Anyway, enough of the bullshit. The next story is about two people who find love. So put your feet up and enjoy…

When an Angel Calls

It was coming up to Christmas and people were shopping around getting presents for their loved ones. I had just stepped out of a restaurant and was looking through a shop window when I felt a tap on the shoulder.

I turned and locked eyes with my sister's husband.

He gave me a warm smile. "I thought it was you! How's it going?"

"I'm good, Lenny! How are you?"

"Can't complain. What are you up to?"

"Just looking around. So, what brings you to these parts?"

"Shopping. But fancy meeting you!"

I told him it was a small world.

"Well, Carrie will be chuffed when I tell her."

I told him not to mention it, but he reminded me that she was my sister.

"She has enough on her plate."

"Don't be silly. She misses you. Why don't you come home with me and say hello."

I told him some other time.

He gave me a funny look. "Did you two have a falling out?"

"We're fine. So, how's the job?" I asked, changing the subject.

"Got a promotion. I'm management now. Got my own office and secretary."

I gave him a pat on the back. "I'm made up for you. You better start cracking that whip."

Lenny laughed and said he was a good boss.

"Good for you."

"And the extra money will come in handy."

"I know where to go when I need a loan."

Lenny laughed. "Well, let me buy the house first. Do you still think about her?"

"Not as much as I ought to."

"It's been two years. Get on with your life. Stop punishing yourself."

I nodded.

"So, what are you doing for Christmas?"

I lied and told him I was working abroad.

"Anywhere nice?"

"Nowhere you'd like to go. Anyway, it was good seeing you, Lenny."

"Well, you know where to find us if you change your mind."

We shook and said Merry Christmas. Then Lenny waved and walked away.

A week went by. I was sitting in a restaurant when I noticed a woman looking at me. She smiled. So, I smiled back. As I was leaving, we met at the door. I opened it to let her past, and she called me a gentleman. We were going the same way. So, we talked while we walked. Her name was Kacey, and she made me laugh. It was something I hadn't done in a long while. So, when she stopped and said goodbye, I tried not to look sad.

"Well, that's me," said Kacey, pointing across the road.

"It was nice talking with you," I told her.
She held out a hand. "Maybe we can do this again."
"I'd like that," I said, shaking it.
"You free next week?"
When I hesitated, she said, "Some other time."
But I said, "Next week would be good. Where?"
"Same place, same time."
"The restaurant?"
She nodded.
"See you then."
Kacey, waved, and walked away.

When I stepped into the restaurant the following week, Kacey was sitting at a table. I went over to join her and sat down.

"So, you've started without me," I told her.

She smiled. "Are you hungry?"

I picked up the menu. "I'm famished. What are we having?"

As if on cue, a waiter appeared. He took our order and went away.

He came back with our meal and a bottle of wine. We thanked him, and he left.

As we ate, we talked and got to know each other.

"So, Dean, why are you still single?"

I told her that I just got over a relationship.

"Do you still see her?"

"She died in a tragic accident."

"Oh, I'm sorry. I didn't mean to…"

"It was a long time ago."

"Well, if you ever want to talk about it."

I shook my head.

Kacey looked at her plate and seemed troubled.

"Is everything alright?" I asked.

"I was just thinking. If it's too soon, we could just—"

But I interrupted her. "I like being here with you."

"You sure?"

"I'm with the most beautiful girl in the world. So, why shouldn't I be?"

She smiled. "Compliments like that will get you a long way. Do you really think I'm beautiful?"

I picked up the bottle and topped up our glasses. "I wouldn't be wasting this wine if I didn't."

She laughed and told me I was funny.

"And here I was thinking I was being romantic."

She raised her glass. "So, what shall we drink to?"

"How about, good friends."

"Good friends," she repeated, and we clinked glasses.

"This is nice."

"Yes, it's nice."

She looked at her plate, raised her head, and stared into my eyes, and we communicated without words. Then we talked for a while. And when it was time to go, I paid the bill and took her home.

When I got up the next morning, I was on a strange bed.

I caught Kacey staring at me.

I asked if everything was alright.

She looked at me with dreamy eyes. "I was just thinking..."

"It must have been painful," I told her.

She gave me a playful slap on the chest. "I was thinking how I would like to kill you!"

"You nearly done that with the sex."

She laughed. "If I remember, you weren't complaining."

"You have the body of an Amazon."

"You're not so bad yourself."

"You say that now but wait till we're married."

She laughed and told me not to get ahead of myself.

"I missed being happy."

"Are we?" she asked.

"What brought that up?"

"I don't want to share you with a ghost."

"You won't."

"Are you sure?"

"She's gone, and I'm with you."

"You sure?"

"I've had time to get over it. Anyway, I want to know about you."

"You've seen me naked, so what's there to know?"

I touched her breasts. "Are these real or man boobs?"

She laughed and slapped my hand. "Are you calling me a man?"

"I was drunk last night. So maybe there's a dick down there."

She put a hand between my legs and grabbed my balls. "Well, right now, Bob's a little horny. Are you ready to go again?"

I rolled on top of her, and we made love.

We spent our days and nights together and time seemed to fly. A week before Christmas, Kacey took me to see a friend. A nice old lady called Rose who had a kind, friendly face. She invited us into her home and took us into the lounge. We sat opposite her on a couch.

She sat on a chair and smiled sweetly at us. "It's nice to meet you, Dean."

I thanked Rose for inviting me.

"I can see why Kacey likes you."

"The feeling's mutual."

Kacey smiled and rubbed my shoulder.

"Kacey has told me a lot about you."

"I hope she was kind."

"I've never seen her happier. So, when are you going to make her an honest woman?"

Kacey nearly choked, making Rose laugh.

"Oh, where are my manners!" She got up suddenly and rushed into the kitchen and came back with lemonade and cake.

We sat round a table, while she poured lemonade into glasses. "Oh, and before I forget, Mary said hello."

When I gave Kacey a look, Rose told me, "It wasn't Kacey."

"Then how?"

"I communicate with the dead."

"You're a medium?"

"Call me a middle person. A conduit between this world and the spirit world."

When I asked Kacey what was going on. She told me to listen to her.

"Please, humour an old lady and tell me what you think about angels."

I told her they were fairytales that mothers told children to help them sleep better at night.

"So, you don't believe in angels?"

"Look at the world today."

"So, you need proof?"

"Are you an angel?" I joked.

"Would it be so hard to believe?"

"Can you prove it?"

"Maybe you should talk with someone else."

There was a shimmering light. Then an apparition appeared before us. At first, I thought my eyes were playing tricks with me. I asked Kacey if she could see it. She squeezed my hand for confirmation.

"Is that really you, Mary?" I cried.

Mary's ghost looked at me and smiled. "How are you, Dean?"

"I thought I'd never see you again!"

"And you with another woman!" said Mary, shaking her head.

Feeling guilty, I dropped Kacey's hand, but she was too dumbstruck to notice.

"But I thought you were gone!"

"I'm joking," said Mary, laughing. Then she said hello to Kacey.

But Kacey just stared at her, speechless.

"The silent kind," said Mary, smiling. "I like her."

I told Mary that I had never stopped loving her.

"And I you, but now you have to let go."

"But what about you?"

"Don't worry about me. I'm in a good place. You have Kacey now. Love her as you would me."

I squeezed Kacey's hand. "Do you mean it?"

"An angel never lies."

"You're an angel?"

"Well, I'm still on probation."

It made us laugh.

"I have to go now," said Mary.

"Wait! What is Heaven like?"

"You'll find out when the time is right, but for now, enjoy the life you have. Bye-bye, everyone."

And before I could say anything, she disappeared.

With Mary gone, I felt sad. Kacey gave me a hug and rubbed my back. "Are you alright, darling?"

I looked into her eyes and kept on staring until a voice broke the silence.

"Now, children, an old lady needs her rest. Run along and be nice to each other. And Merry Christmas."

We returned the compliment, thanked our host, and went on our merry way. As we were walking along the street, I asked Kacey if I had imagined it.

"I saw it too. Maybe we should go to church and no sex before marriage."

I told Kacey I was a believer not an idiot, and we both started laughing.

So, we got married, had three beautiful children and lived happily ever after. What happened in-between? Well, that's another story. Maybe I'll share it with you one day. But before I go, I would like to dedicate a song to Kacey. 'Greatest Love Story' by an artist called Lanco. I know, call me a softie but you should never give up on love.

END

Well, folks, it's been fun but, as they say, all good things must come to an end. So, I'll just mosey on out. Has anyone seen my horse? Well, Grim Reapers, thanks for being a swell audience, but got to run. I ate a burrito, and my arse is killing me. "Lordy! Lordy!" So, until we meet again. See you soon with more madcap humour. Hey, don't shoot the messenger. I'm just passing it on for a friend. Did I mention that my friend's an alien from another planet. Hey, who's bullshitting who?

What's that, you want to go crazy with a crazy guy? Well let's go, fucker! You and me! But first let me take this tab. Shit, brother, I'm back in Vietnam! Alright, adios, amigo, I'm gone. I was never here. Oh, and don't forget to turn off the laughing gas. Bye-bye, suckers.

A guy was on a health kick. Always exercising, had no time to enjoy himself. Bottled water and healthy living. Two years later, he got knocked down by a lorry.
　At the inquest, the driver told the judge, "He came out of nowhere!"
　Judge asked, "Didn't he see you?"
　"He was looking at his fitness watch."

One guy was bitching about money problems. So, I told him if you're throwing your money away on water you can get free from a tap, no wonder you have money problems.

"Hey, buddy, can you give me a scoop?"
　"Yeah, don't write bullshit."

Remember the love of your life. The one you want to grow old with. Eight years later, you're sitting in front of the telly with a beer, a fat gut, and a pipe. "Baby, get me another beer!"
　Baby's standing behind you, playing with a knife. "I left a good man for that fucker and all he does is drink, watch telly, and tell jokes!"

Three guys are on a hospital ward lying in a coma. The doctor walks into the ward, points to the first bed, and asks the nurse, "How long has he been here?"

She tells him a year. He points to the next bed, two years, and the next, three years. So, he tells her to wheel the third guy into the operating room and they give him a brain transplant. The guy wakes up from his coma and looks around. "Where am I?" They tell him a hospital. So, he points at the face in the mirror, and says, "And who's that ugly bastard?"

The Power of Words

Many of us don't realize how effective words are. Especially in the poor communities. To communicate and be understood. Learning how to articulate our language so we may put our meaning across. The power of words is an invaluable tool. We need words to express our thoughts and ideas and explain how we feel. Lacking the ability can often lead to frustration, misunderstanding, confusion, and in many cases confrontations. I've been in many situations where I couldn't defend myself because of a poor vocabulary, and in any dispute, it's usually the strongest argument that wins. And a clever argument is a convincing argument. Like in our courts of law.

In many underprivileged areas people lack a decent education because of a poor quality of life. So, they are treated unfairly and suffer injustice because they lack the understanding and meaning of words. I left school at 15 with no qualifications. I was backward and couldn't read and write. So, I learned the hard way how being illiterate can impair your life. So, I taught myself to read and write.

I remember when I was a child saying goodbye to the house where I grew up. It was like leaving a part of myself behind. Abandoning a friend. I walked away with a heavy heart. So, I decided to write a poem…

This old house, damped, soiled, and stained,
Through years that passed and came,
Its body old, decrepit bones and feeble flesh,
Its weak doors held a sour scent of ill.
Deranged and cold, a lonely hole,
Where the dossers come to dwell,
Beyond the wasted age, and years of tainted love.

Are you ready for some love. "Hey, baby, go easy on that tequila. That's my welfare cheque you're drinking."

Have you ever been in love? Silly question. I remember my first time. It was a first date. I was shaking so much. She thought I was a quadriplegic. She asked if I was alright. I told her I hadn't taken my medication. I thought the joke would break the ice. She gave me that look.

"I'll just go and powder my nose. I'll be right back."

I didn't see her again. Anyway, no hard feelings. Many years later, it still haunts me. Well, I've dedicated this poem to you...

Fools in Love

Midnight wind is blowing, stars are shinning bright,
Man meets a woman in the coldness of the night,
He whispers to her softly, and looks into her eyes,
And tells her that he loves her,
now the moment is just right,
But unbelieving is this woman as she cries and
holds him tight,
For in her heart's a whisper,
"Please don't tell me lies."

The Comfortable Preacher

I used to live in a small village that was shy of 1000 people. It was miles from anywhere, and there were no trains or buses. If you didn't have a car, you had to rely on cabs, and they made a fortune ripping people off. If you're stuck in the middle of nowhere, what are you going to do? There was only a Co-op, a village hall, two pubs, two churches, and a museum. The nearest doctors were 20 miles away, and many of the residents were elderly.

"Doctor! I'm getting chest pains! I think I'm having a heart attack!"

"Make sure you have some cab fare."

It was a desperate affair. Everyone was robbing you, even the council. I was living in a council building with around 30 flats. It had a warden, but the warden was always off sick, and when we did see her, she was always nipping out for a smoke. It was like the job was killing her. It was supposed to be a kind of retirement home, but it was more like a nut house for the mentally deranged. There was some crazy guy that kept giving me a hard time. He drank and wouldn't take his meds. In the end, they had to take him away. When the white coats came, everyone were hiding in their flats like they were afraid to be next. And people were always bickering and complaining about each other like they were criminals. It was insulting. I had Netflix, and I told one resident that you didn't need a license for it. She called the police on me anyway. In the year and a half, I was there, four people had died. I got out of there before I was next.

And the two churches in the village were All Saints, and Baptist. I tried the Baptist church for a while to be a part of the community, but the priest was holier-than-thou. He was living like a fat king in a nice house his parishioners got him. It was like a mansion. You walk past his house and the lights were blaring in every room. Never mind the recession. He even had a big family getting fat off them, and he was telling everyone to give up their possessions and follow him on a long hard road of sacrifice. Like he was saving the hungry. "Your reward will be in Heaven!" And he even described Heaven in all its wonderous glory like he had been there. Well, maybe he should set an example. Give up that fine house and take his mission to the poor. If 'hard sell' was a subject in school, that guy would be a master at it. He even had the flock believing they were sheep. I was just waiting for them to bleat.

Don't get me wrong, I'm not calling him a bad person. Just pompous and self-serving. He had a narrow-minded view of the world and judged everyone by his own standards. The community was his world. This peaceful and uneventful village. And the priest cared more about his status in the community than the people in it. He was always trying to impress people with his superior knowledge. Even when he didn't have the answer to something, he would make it up.

When I talked about the plight of poor people in bad areas, he had little sympathy for them. They had brought it on themselves. They were going to Hell. He wouldn't be so high and mighty if he were in their shoes. People like to judge, but that sucker had never known pain and suffering. But he had the cheek to sit on his high horse and condemn people who couldn't help themselves. And he called himself a Christian? And that sucker had an answer for everything.

I asked him, "The scientists say that we evolved from primates, ape-like creatures, and you're saying Adam and Eve. Who's right and who's wrong?"

He told me, "The scientists don't know what they're talking about." Like their evidence was bullshit.

So, I asked him, "Adam and Eve had Cain and Abel, and Cain and Abel met two girls. Where did the girls come from?"

He couldn't come up with an answer, so he told me I shouldn't question the Bible. Yeah, tell that to your sheep. They tell us stories about Adam and Eve, and how we shouldn't think for ourselves, but that's only to control us.

I couldn't talk with that joker. He had an answer for everything. Like he was the wisest man on Earth. Maybe there is something good up there, but it's not how he describes it. I also believe that we are not alone in the universe. That there is intelligent life on other worlds but try telling that to a priest. It would destroy their concept of religion. "It's bad enough having to share the planet with each other, but aliens from other worlds!" Anyway, each to their own.

— *End* —

Two aliens sitting on a rock, thinking about somewhere nice to go for their holiday, and one of them says, "Don't go to Earth."

Malcolm X wanted a separate state for Blacks, and to fight fire with fire, but Martin Luther King wanted peace and integration. A world where people of all nations could live together, learn from one another, and tolerate our differences. Holy people talk about kindness, forgiveness, and compassion, and how they are destined for the Promised Land, then encourage others to hate and kill and contradict what they preach. Words are only words if you can't practise what you preach. I believe in the principles of good. And peace among all nations. But if you can't make your peace on Earth, how will you find it in Heaven? And ask yourself another question. If Heaven is a place without hate, violence, and discrimination, that has compassion and kindness, what kind of people would God want in it? You can pray all you like but if you haven't got love and kindness in your heart then it doesn't mean a thing. You say that God is good, and he knows everything. Well, he knows you.

When I was a child, I remember going to a school that had a bad reputation for fighting. You either got tough or were bullied. And the kids were always stealing and nicking cars. It was how I learned to drive. Joking! The teachers were reluctant to teach us. They got back nothing but grief. So they went through the motions, but many didn't have the heart for the job. Anyway, the kids were too dumb to learn. The only education they got at home was telly, football, and boxing. I hated school and couldn't wait to get out. Those first years make a big impression on our lives.

Black Boy Joe

I sat in the classroom, alone and afraid,
While all the other children, spat at me,
Laughed at me, and called me nasty little names,
Alone in the back with my humiliation and shame,
While the ugly honky faces called me wog,
nigger and coon.
The teacher just sat there at the head of the class,
Ignoring the banter and the evil vile songs,
With his head in a book as if nothing was wrong,
As they mocked me, and jeered,
and the derision went on,
I trembled and cried and couldn't take anymore,
Hated myself and wished I had never been born.

I grew up in London in the 1970s with a far-right group called The National Front. They were cowards and bullies, spreading lies about Black people, and getting others to hate us. It was shameful! They blamed the Blacks for everything. If you lost your job or couldn't get one, a Black person stole it off you. If a white woman got involved with a Black guy, she was a traitor and a whore. And white people would treat her like scum. They even had the police thinking we were the enemy. The country was in trouble, so we were the cause. It was alright in the 1950s when they needed us to do the dirty work.

Now we were a burden on the country. I remember the 1970s when Thatcher created the sus law. If a crime was committed, the cops would convince the victims it was a Black guy. It didn't matter if he was in a wheelchair. If he was Black, he did it. Wherever we went, there was a target on our back. When I left London, people were different. They didn't see me for the colour of my skin. They accepted me for who I was.

That was many years ago, and these are supposed to be better times, but in some places, people still carry grudges. So, when I hear about the far-right getting up to their old tricks in places like London, it makes me think about the injustice in this country. Anyway, here's a poem about a Black kid getting stopped on the street...

Questions

Questions I heard,
when the police stopped me on the road,
Questions I heard,
as they baffled me with lies,
Questions I heard,
as they told me of my crime,
Questions, more questions,
as they took me for a ride.
Dogs like you commit the crimes,
Dogs like you that waste our time,
Dogs like you are just one kind,
Dogs like you must toe the line.
Questions I heard,
when they took me to the court,
Questions I heard,
as I stood there in the dock,
Questions I heard,
if, and when, and why?
Questions, more questions,
as my mum began
to cry.

In England, it's like we're living in a continuous loop, repeating ourselves, day after day. And many turn to alcohol and drugs to get over their monotonous lives.

And people fool themselves that they are happy, but the mental health problems in this country tell another story.

In England, we are famous for our pubs. The British pride themselves on their drinking habits. They boast about their achievements, but there's one thing the British can be proud of. Our stupidity.

I was in a pub with one guy. He was telling me that he functioned better when he drank and kept falling off the stool. Last bell, he was going through his pockets. "Now where did I put my car keys?" Anyway...

We Reap What We Sow

A crowded world of selfish people,
riding boats, year after year,
A boat the government will carry to
a land of yet more tears.
And while we're capable of learning,
and while the luxuries are here,
Man will always be bone idle
as to live on someone's fear.
Some think life is all too pointless,
some think judgement day is near,
Would suicide be a way out in
this depressing atmosphere.
Is this what our lives consist of,
getting by on booze and drugs,
Getting high on sex and violence and
learning aids on how to kill.

It's a crazy time when we see children committing senseless acts of violence, and it's happening more and more every day. How did we get to this? Are people born bad or does society condition us to be bad? Some like to blame it on what is going on around the world, but it's happening on our doorstep. And when I look around and see ordinary folks spreading hate, hostility and violence against innocent people, it makes me wonder about the kind of society that we are living in where discrimination and prejudice are condoned by people that claim to be civilized. But, like karma, what goes around comes around. People respond to how they are treated, and it creates a toxic and poisonous environment. It's why in many overcrowded cities the tension is like a pressure cooker waiting to explode. All it takes is a spark like the hate riots in London. An excuse for people to release their anger and frustrations. It doesn't matter who the victim is, long as they have someone to blame. Anyway, this is a poem about a boy that rebelled against his environment, called…

Bad Boy

Ugly and scarred, you yearned to be loved,
You kept searching for kindness,
but the world can be cruel.
It seems so unfair to be judged by your looks,
Rejected and shunned, to be last in the queue.
So, you learned to be bad, lied, cheated, and stole,
Because money's a language only fools understand.
You had to be hard, never mind those you hurt,
You can't afford to be nice when you're looking at jail.
Now you're respected and feared, heartless and cold,
And not blind to the ways of a devious world.

Respect for the Dead

I wore my uniform in honour of a dear departed friend. The widow of the deceased, a frail figure in black, wept quietly into her handkerchief as people filed passed offering their sympathy and condolences. Part of her had died, words could not express the hollow loneliness for his cruel desertion, but grace and dignity denied her from displaying any emotions other than what was required. Many of the faces were that of strangers, people who claimed to be friends of the man she never knew.

When the ceremony ended, the priest concluded, "He was a good man who will no doubt find his reward in Heaven…"

As he looked around to take in each of the faces gathered in mournful silence, people bowed and made the sign of the cross. Then the coffin was lowered into the ground, and flowers were placed around the grave.

As the widow walked away, people smiled and touched her arm, once again offering their condolences.

She made her way to a car by the cemetery gates. The chauffeur, an old man in a black suit and cap, opened the rear door for his lone passenger, who entered without seeming to be aware of him. Then the car crept away from the curb, followed by others, and was gone.

I watched the last one go, then took off my hat, knelt by the grave and placed flowers on the headstone. "So, long, buddy, see you in the next life. Rest in peace." Then I got up, put on my hat, and walked away.

End

People will knock you down and get satisfaction in seeing you fall. Show them that you are better than them by improving your mind.

Discovering who I am

When I was a child, I never had much of an education because I was different than the other kids. I couldn't learn like them, fit in or belong because of my autism. But I had to pretend to be like them so I wouldn't seem out of place. When you're a child it's confusing not knowing what is going on in your head and being unable to make sense of the world. I was on my own and had to figure it out for myself. Someone once told me that I had a chemical imbalance in my brain. At the time, I didn't put much stock in it, but now it kind of makes sense. If the chemicals in our brains are different, our brains would be wired different and would be considered abnormal. Some have even called it a sickness. A psychotic disorder. But autism isn't a sickness. It's a disability and should be treated with understanding and kindness. Not medication.

For as long as I can remember, I've been diagnosed with a mental illness, but I was watching a programme on Netflix about people with autism and the challenges they faced and found myself identifying with them. They were normal, happy people, living ordinary lives because of the nice people around them, and it made me feel comfortable about myself. Because of my condition, I had all these confusing thoughts racing through my brain, making me anxious and scared. So, I drank alcohol to relax, but I became too dependent on it. I saw doctors, but my mind was a mess, and I didn't know how to express my thoughts. So, they diagnosed me schizophrenia because my mother and sister had it. So, it made sense that I had it too, even though I wasn't hearing voices or having psychotic thoughts. So, they prescribed me chlorpromazine, doxepin and tranquillizers. Chlorpromazine for psychotic disorder, and doxepin for depression and anxiety, and sleeping pills and Valium. But it only made it worse. The anxiety was so severe, I started having heart palpitations and muscle seizures. I was sweating all the time, and I was nervous and anxious. But when I went back to the doctors, they treated me like it was all in my head. Like I was making it up. It was hurtful, humiliating, and frustrating. So, I started going less. Then COVID happened and we had to distance ourselves because of the virus. So, I stopped taking the medication. I was warned against it, but years later, despite not taking the drugs, I am in better health. Both mentally and physically. And I can function with a clearer mind.

Much of my life have been wasted putting my faith in doctors. Trusting the medical experts to find a cure for my behavioural problems. But my state of mind wasn't an illness. It was a condition that required understanding and care. Yet I was made to feel as if I was crazy. By the doctors, and everyone around me. And I hated myself. I remember being a child. The kids thought I was strange and treated me cruelly. So, I avoided school. And, as a result, my education had suffered. But, later, when I understood the value of an education. I taught myself. It was a difficult challenge, and at times, I was ready to quit, but I was determined to learn. I wanted to be better. Someone once told me, why do we need words, when we can communicate with our actions. Words are the basis of our understanding. It's how we explain how things work. We need words to express our thoughts and ideas.

A little while ago, I wanted to know more about being autistic. So, I made an application with the medical people, which meant going back to the GP. So, I spoke to a woman in my surgery, and she arranged for me to see someone. But there's a two to three years waiting list. So, I thought, *why bother?* I'm 62, and I've gone this long without help. Why should I need them now?

A lot has happened in my life. I've been 62 years on this planet. How do you put it all into context? I should have left this world many times, but it's always felt like there was a guardian angel watching me, seeing me fall, picking me up and helping me learn from my mistakes. Don't get me wrong, I'm no saint, but I have a decent enough heart. I've been an idiot and got things wrong, but it was never intentional. My life could have gone in any direction, but I had luck and a little sense. Especially where booze was involved. Alcohol can get you into a lot of trouble. I knew a bloke that got into a drunken fight and ended up in prison for manslaughter. The guy he hit whacked his head on the pavement and died from a concussion. So, he spent several years behind bars regretting what he had done. But you can't turn back the clock. One stupid mistake can ruin your life forever. So, I try to think about the consequences of my actions. There's a rule I take seriously. Avoid bad company and wrong places. But failing that, a calm head and a thoughtful word will get you a lot further than a violent confrontation. And, no, I am not quoting Al Capone. Still, who am I giving advice? I should be taking lessons from you.

So, you've read a few books and think you're an authority on autism but put yourself in my shoes. My mother and father came on a boat from Dominica to England in 1962. Mother was pregnant with me. I was born a few months later in Woolwich hospital in London. And shortly after, we moved to the Old Kent Road. My primary school was just across the road, and Millwall football stadium was on our street. On a weekend, you'd hear the supporters going past our door, singing and shouting, but they were just boys. Those were innocent times. We had a garden and an outside toilet. And a train track was just above it. You'd hear the trains going to and from Central London. I had two older brothers and a sister back in Dominica. They came over when I was nine. We weren't close, so I won't talk about them. I haven't seen them in thirty years, so I don't know if they're still alive. And forget Father. He was a womanizer and liked to bash us around. And he enjoyed a drink. Maybe the booze made him angry. Who knows what was in his mind? I only knew he was a horrible man. So, I hid from him whenever I could. But that's another story. Mother didn't deserve that man. So, when he left us for another woman, it was the happiest day of my life. I thought Christmas had come early, but Mother started drinking and smoking, had a breakdown and ended up in a mental institution. They said it was schizophrenia. I remember coming home from school and seeing her talk to the walls. They'd be bottles around, and she'd be drinking and smoking. Anyway, they came and took her away. Back in those days, they didn't know much about schizophrenia. So, they locked her in an institution and drugged her up like a zombie. So, she wouldn't be a nuisance to the staff.

When I saw her, she couldn't even recognize her own son. It broke me up. They kept her for a long while, and when they let her out, she drank and smoked herself to death. It was 1994, a month before Christmas, and she had just turned 60. Anyway, she's in a better place now. If there's a God up there, I know he's looking after her. Back then, like autism, they didn't know much about schizophrenia, but today we have a better understanding.

The doctors wrote me off as having schizophrenic tendency. Which is an odd because 'tendency doesn't' specify that I have the disease. It just indicates that my behaviour resembles it, but I don't hear voices or have psychotic thoughts. So, what is their definition of the disease? They like to confuse you with medical jargon, so you don't read too much into it. And who's going to question the doctors with all their medical knowledge? They can do whatever they want. Ask Harold Shipman. So, I got sent to a psychiatrist, but the psychiatrist knew nothing about autism. So, he sent me back to the doctor. And the doctor gave me more pills. And I trusted them, but what did I know. Back then, if you'd asked me what autism was, I'd have thought it was some exotic fruit. Then I saw a movie called *Mercury Rising*, about a kid that was good with numbers, and I thought they were geniuses, and I couldn't even read and write. Then, recently, I saw a series on Netflix called *Spectrum* about autistic people and realized that we shared similar characteristics.

My life has been spent travelling around the country from one slum landlord to the next. When you're unemployed your living options are limited. So, you take what you get. I've been lumbered with violent neighbours, crazy people, and troublemakers. All the undesirables that the government deem unworthy to be among decent folks. And when you live like an animal you think like an animal. It's the law of the jungle. Alright, people drink and take drugs to cope with their miserable lives, but many lose their shit and take it out on innocent people. I stay away from those fuckers. They're their own worst enemies. Occasionally, you get a good landlord, but the majority try to rip you off. They put you in squalid conditions and cause trouble if you complain. And many won't do the repairs. And if you don't like it, there're plenty of mugs to take your place. I had one landlord that wanted me to go to jail for him. He was having trouble with a neighbour and wanted me to sort him out. I told him I was busy. Then he got others to give me a hard time. I got out of there and went somewhere else. Where the natives are friendly.

I might look a good size, but I'm nobody's fool. And they say the tenants have rights, but who are they going to go to? You or the council? And the council's on the side of the landlord. We're just scum. You're at the bottom of the heap. And in many of the places, the windows and doors are paper thin. You can hear the traffic outside and people breathing next door, and some are so small, you'd have more space in a shed. And some have shared toilets and showers, and dirty bastards that won't clean them. It's a desperate situation. You hear all the bullshit about people's rights, but when you're poor and unemployed, you're on your own. And they wonder why people work the system. I've seen bailiffs turf families on the street. Those sadistic bastards take pleasure in their work. They have no scruples about evicting babies. And in some of the places the conditions are so bad, you end up with serious health problems and mental illness. And you wonder why people choose to sleep rough on the street. A quarter of the country's population are on mental welfare because of the unfit conditions that society imposes on us.

So, some drink and take drugs to lessen the pain. And you can get cheap booze in any shop. You buy a newspaper, there are bottles of cider on the shelve. "I'll have a newspaper and a bottle of White Lightning." The kids are even starting early. If their parents are drunks, it must be okay. In some areas, you're only popular if you drink. And the fatality rate is appalling. Booze is one of the biggest killers in this country, but the government don't want to cure the problem. They want to encourage it because of the taxes it brings. And wherever there's money, there's corruption. So, the government throw us the occasional sweetener to win our hearts, then it's back to the old ways. I read once about a politician who went on the street for a night to live among the homeless, then went back to his cushy life and told everyone that he knew what it was like to be homeless. Like he had seen the light. One night with Jesus doesn't make you a saint. I could see him sitting on his yacht patting himself on the back. Go back to posing on the social media. It's more convincing. So, when a doctor claims he understands me. I can see right through their bullshit. When I needed help, all I got were pills.

I was reading the other day about an Australian guy that killed six people because he couldn't get a girlfriend. If he has thoughts like that, no wonder he couldn't get a girlfriend. And you call me crazy. I remember watching a Guy Ritchie movie called *Snatch*, where they were joking about England. A mob guy leaves England and gets on a plane to New York. At the airport, they ask him, "Anything to declare?"

He tells them, "Don't go to England."

Around COVID, I stopped taking the medication. Some years have passed, and I haven't gone crazy. Maybe it's a miracle. The side effects have gone, and my mind is good. Wait, I'll get back to you on that. Joking! I avoid trouble and stressful situations, and enjoy reading and writing, watching boxsets and movies, and listening to music of all genres. It's therapeutic and helps me relax. You should never limit your mind.

Growing up, I never had a family. Well, not in a traditional sense. There was no love or affection. It was like living in a house with strangers. Anyway, it's behind me. All that matters is here and now. The last time I saw my family was around 1994. About 30 years ago, when Mother passed away. We had nothing to say to each other, and didn't say goodbye. Some things are best forgotten.

I've had my ups and downs. It's been a struggle and an education, but life has taught me what doesn't defeat you, makes you stronger. It's meeting the right people, walking the right path, and learning from our mistakes. It's how we grow and become better people. And if my 62 years on this planet has taught me anything, it's how to survive.

(Michael David)